S0-AIY-557

HEART OF AN ASSASSIN

Laura Pauling

Redpoint Press
Heart of an Assassin: Circle of Spies, Book 2
Copyright 2012 Laura Pauling
Second e-book edition, 2013
Second paperback edition, 2013

All rights reserved. No part of this publication may be
reproduced, stored in a retrieval system or transmitted in any form
or by any means, electronic, mechanical, photocopying, recording
or otherwise without the prior written consent of the copyright
holder, except for brief passages in connection with a review
written for inclusion in a magazine, newspaper, blog or broadcast.

This is a work of fiction, and is produced from the author's
imagination. People, places and things mentioned in this novel are
used in a fictional manner.

Summary: Savvy finally reunites with Malcolm, the hot
assassin she fell for in Paris. No longer the accidental spy, Savvy
strikes a dangerous deal with a family of assassins and must
complete a series of deadly missions.

Edited by TS Tate
Cover design by Novak Illustration

ebook ISBN: 978-0-9852327-2-6
paperback ISBN: 978-0-9852327-3-3

Visit http://laurapauling.com.

Dedication

For all my friends, writers and my team who made this possible. And thanks to all the readers. May you find adventure inside this book and in life.

One

THE COLD SENSATION STARTED as an itch on the back of my neck, like a spider crawling. The imaginary legs tap, tap, tapping against my skin, the tiny hairs bristling and tickling.

I shivered then shrugged it off, blaming it on a cold draft. I was thankful the hood of my sweatshirt kept my face in shadows. My hands were jammed in the front pocket, my fingers running over and over the smooth casing of a pocketknife.

Mom told me to infiltrate the market place of our seacoast village in Greece. She wanted me to study five people to determine their economic status, why they were shopping, if they were happy or not, their age, marital status, the color of their underwear, blah, blah, blah.

I'd been doing this every week for the last few months when I really wanted to jump from planes or attend fancy parties as a seductive spy and duel with swords in the dark

1

shadows. Cool things. I was tired of observing people haggle over the price of a radish.

But ever since my adventures in Paris, where I solved the mystery of my best friend's disappearance and rescued a prisoner from captivity all while outwitting a family of assassins—yeah, ever since all that, Mom had been a wee bit overprotective.

I drew closer to the crowded streets, totally incognito in my average teen girl clothing, and took in the increasing chatter of the crowds: the deep bellows of merchants trying for a sale, the whine of toddlers begging for some shiny toy or piece of candy, and the quiet hum of ongoing conversation. Beaded jewelry twinkled in the sun, glitter on T-shirts flashed, and friendship bracelets and handmade necklaces hung in a variety of brilliant colors. I searched for my first target and for something sweet to snack on while I observed.

I found the sweet dessert first. After I paid the man, I cradled the pastry in the palm of my hand. The wafer thin layers with walnuts were soaked in sweet honey syrup and tasted absolutely delicious.

The itch on the back of my neck grew to a prickle and the spider crawled down my back. This time I couldn't ignore it or blame weather patterns, and my hoodie didn't offer much protection or camouflage. I quickened my pace, the need to hide rising above my training mission. I ducked one way, then scooted between two old ladies, but the feeling remained. Someone's eyes were on me.

No one knew Mom and I were hiding out in Greece, but I made constant sweeps of the thickening crowds and pushed through the old, the young and the in-between. A lady with her messy hair piled on her head hassled a seller for a lower price on lettuce. As the seller ran fingers through his bushy black hair and argued, I inched backwards under the shade of his tent. Hiding. Hoping that no one noticed me.

Heat flushed my body and instinct screamed at me to get home. Fast. Each person who looked in my direction caused my heart rate to triple. I took several meditative deep breaths and merged with the crowd, acting like I suspected nothing. I bought a head of lettuce, and held onto it like it could protect me in a fight. I moved to the next cart and bought onions, even though Mom can't stand them. At the next cart, I used the last of the change and bought fresh flowers, then robotically turned and moved toward home, past the fresh produce and back into the touristy carts. As I moved from the thicker crowds and turned onto a side street, my body tensed. Footsteps fell in line behind me.

I stopped and slowly turned, ready to take them out with whatever method I could even if I had to bombard the guy with onions or offer up my dessert in exchange for my freedom. That would totally work on me.

3

I certainly didn't expect the Rastafarian teen who looked like he didn't belong here anymore than I did. Long brown dreadlocks hid his face. He banged his head and swayed to the beat pounding in his ears through his ear buds. No guns. No black clothing or hulking men out to get me.

He made beat box noises and drummed his legs with his hands. I froze, feeling stupid staring at his matted hair for no good reason. When he moved into my personal space, I freaked out and couldn't convince my legs to run home. So much for a glorious confrontation. I tightened my grip on my pastry, ready to smash-in-the-face and run.

He rocked out, and just inches from me, turned his back. "Don't act like you know me or that I'm talking to you."

Feelings that I'd kept pressed down bubbled up and spilled over, washing me with memories. Paris. Kissing. Rushing through the streets of the Extravaganza. Malcolm. For some reason my vocal chords wouldn't cooperate and I said nothing.

He kept his back to me, pretending to listen to music. He said nothing while a mother strode by with her three children. My breaths came faster and faster. There was only one reason he would be in disguise and talking to me so secretly. Someone was following him or following me. Probably his family. As in his older brother, Will, the one who put a bullet in my leg in Paris. I had known it was a

4

possibility, but this made it real. This was not how I imagined our reunion. And all my thoughts about wanting excitement felt like a complete lie.

"We need to talk," he said. "Tomorrow night, near the docks you'll find a bunch of sailboats. Find the one almost at the end. Both sails will be down and Mozart will be playing. I'll be waiting."

Then as if he was a one-man band he drummed his hands against his legs and moved on down the street until he rounded the corner. I sank my teeth into the pastry, letting the caramelized sweetness distract me from the many thoughts running through my brain. But one in particular managed to break through and repeat.

Malcolm had found me.

Two

THE NEXT DAY, MOM cooked dinner while I schemed on how to slip out unnoticed. Perfume lingered around her as she served up the chicken stir-fry and her every move sent a scent of apple blossoms my way. Her hair was up in an elegant twist, no strands framing her face; too sharp and clean cut for a dinner with her daughter. The fresh flowers I'd bought the day before wilted in a glass vase at our small table. She hadn't understood why I came home with onions and flowers.

"So what's with the fancy hairdo?" I asked.

Mom patted her twist to make sure it was secure and then placed the serving dish on the table and retrieved the plates from the cupboard. "Can't I make dinner for my daughter without being questioned?"

"Sure." I served up the stir-fry and stabbed my fork into my mushy veggies, wishing they were a giant brownie.

We didn't say much during dinner. There were too many unanswered questions and fears piling up in my mind. Mom cleaned up her plate down to the last zucchini. She glanced at her watch and brought her plate over to the sink. "I'll be heading out for a bit."

No surprise there. "Want company?"

"Not tonight." She hummed and rinsed off her plate. "What are you going to do?"

Mom was good at that. Answering an awkward question and then redirecting the attention back on me. So I'd forget. But I never did.

I stretched my arms out to the side and let out a totally fake yawn. "I think I'll shower and head to bed with a book. I'm kinda tired."

"Okay. Have a good night. If you could clean up that would be great." Mom kissed the top of my head, grabbed a shawl and was out the door.

Three minutes after I scrubbed the dishes, I was too. It wasn't easy making my way through the village in the dark of night. Every unknown sound creeped me out: the scurry of tiny animals in the brush, the creak of tree limbs in the breeze, and the slight echo of traffic from the main roads. I rushed down to the docks feeling only one step ahead of my invisible enemies, darting from streetlight to streetlight until I realized it was probably better to stick with the shadows. Every sound was the footstep of an evil monk with the gleam of murder twinkling in his eye or the pitter-patter of

Malcolm's brother with a sniper aimed and ready. My entire back turned into knots.

The briny smell of the Mediterranean tickled my nose, and I slowed down. When the tips of sailboats reflecting the moon caught my eye, I crept along until I was on the dock. My feet created a dull thudding noise on the wooden slats. The sway of the structure made me feel off kilter and slightly sick. Dark water lapped against the sides of the boats. I felt exposed, a sitting duck waiting to be picked off.

"Psst. Hey, Savvy!"

I jumped and whirled around, my heart rate spiking. Then I heard the strain of violin music and calmed down. If someone was going to put me six feet under they wouldn't call my name, they'd just do it. I peered through the darkness. "Malcolm?"

"Yeah. Come on in."

He stood on deck, light spilling out the door to his cabin. His familiar shape, the outline of his face and the hard lines of his body caused a twang in my chest, and parts of me I hadn't known were hollow for six months filled with warmth and anticipation. His words whispered to me by the River Seine returned. He cared about me. Or he had. I flashed him a nervous smile and stepped aboard.

Down in the cabin, we stood too close for comfort, looking everywhere but at each other. A tiny table was built into the side, a convenient kitchen tucked into the corner, and a door at the end led into what looked like it might be a bedroom.

"Do you live here?" I asked, running my fingers along the manly curtains with no frill, thinking how my mom would disapprove of the layer of dust on the sill.

"Yeah, I'm taking a little break from the family. You know."

"Totally." I couldn't control my head as it bobbed up and down. I didn't know much at all about his family and he probably knew everything about mine. I wanted to look at him, study his face and find the tiny dimple on his right cheek, see if he had changed like I had, but I could only make it to his feet and his frayed flip-flops. And his feet pretty much looked the same from what I could remember.

"When I couldn't follow through with my mission in Paris, they didn't make it easy for me." He stretched and totally failed in acting nonchalant about the whole thing.

I gasped and met his eyes, fighting off the fluttery feeling in my stomach. His words were laden with hidden hurts, secrets about his family I'd probably never learn. "They kicked you out?"

"Not exactly. I could've stayed but the looks from my dad and Will's obnoxious remarks were getting to me. I had to get out of there."

This time I nodded with complete understanding. I knew something about living with tension, but I didn't have a family boat to escape too. Must be nice.

"Want something to drink?" he asked and ran his fingers across the top of a cooler.

"No thanks."

The conversation stalled and seconds ticked by that felt like hours. I couldn't stand the silence so I searched for a story, any story.

"You should've seen my first day in the market place." I waved my hand and fake laughed. "I turned down a zillion streets like I was in some sort of mythical labyrinth and never found what I was looking for even though I stumbled upon a few touristy stands and wanted to buy some twinkly jewelry until finally I had to ask this old guy, who I think was a bit drunk, how to get back home and you should've seen this guy's hair, streaked with white, a total bed head."

My flow of words slowed to a trickle when I ran out of breath while the burn of embarrassment crept up the back of my neck. Tension separated us like a brick wall. What happened to the easy conversation we'd had in Paris? I'd spent months thinking, dreaming, and wondering about him. And here he was, right in front of me, and we were like strangers. I went through my inventory of lame jokes. Something. Anything to fill the widening gap between us. But mostly I just bit my lip to stop another stupid story from leaking out.

Malcolm sprawled across a padded bench, his long legs taking up most of it, and he studied me, his charcoal-flecked eyes pulling at me, questioning. Deep inside me, embedded in the walls of my heart, I felt a flicker, a tiny spark of what I used to feel.

"So," I said, crumpling on the inside and wishing this moment would end.

"So," he repeated, then straightened up, a slight glint in his eyes. "How've you been?"

I skipped any more stories and reverted back to what we knew. Paris. The glib reply came easily. "You mean after you left me in an, um, rather uncomfortable position under the Eiffel Tower?"

"Payback's a bitch." He grinned.

Feeling sparked again, and I couldn't help but smile back. "I've been just fine and dandy. Mom scooped me up and we moved here to recover. Been living here ever since."

"No, I mean in general," he said.

"Oh. I'm fine." I threw the remark out there, leaning against the sidewall and crossing my legs, hoping, praying I looked cool, like meeting up with him was part of any other day.

"You seem different," he said and tapped his fingers together as if they itched to hold some kind of weapon.

I patted the palm of my hands against my legs and shrugged, rolling off the past five months like they were nothing. "Life happens."

"I understand."

His eyes caught mine and I knew he truly did understand. If anyone could understand about not fitting in with family, the longing to be accepted, and the need to be told the truth once in a while, it was Malcolm.

He stood and stepped closer, not saying anything. I stared at his chin and the tiny hairs that needed to be shaved. I couldn't get myself to look into his eyes again or at his mouth. My insides quivered. His hand traced my arm through my sweatshirt and he tugged on the sleeve, pulling me closer. I stumbled a bit. All I wanted was to lift my head and feel his lips on mine, a chance I thought I'd never have again, but how would this ever work? A spy and an assassin? Impossible.

"Look at me," he said gently.

I kept my eyes to his chest. The feelings battled within me, part of me wanting to reach out and touch him, the other part urging me to run before I could get hurt, before Mom found out.

His breath whispered against my skin, pulling my head up. I found his eyes, the charcoal flecks welcoming me home.

I found compassion and understanding. I found a lost friend. The temperature in the room skyrocketed and a rush of emotion flooded my heart, drowning out any logic in keeping back the old feelings I had for this boy. Suddenly it didn't matter that six months had passed. Time warped and I felt it was just yesterday we were whispering and laughing together. Forgotten memories and feelings welled, pushing to the surface, and I struggled to hide them.

He kissed my forehead and I pulled away, joking. "You'd better watch it. My Greek bodyguard could board your small sailboat at any time."

A devilish grin creeping across his face told me he wasn't giving up. "Sure." He said it like he didn't believe me.

"Seriously. I really shouldn't be here," I whispered.

He knew what I meant. We were fine until he brought me home to meet the family considering they were trying to wipe out my family line. Permanently. They'd already tried to once. In Paris. The only reason I'd survived was because Malcolm was captured by my cute looks and couldn't pull the trigger. Either that or he just chickened out. I liked to think it was my cute looks and infectious smile.

"Shh. Let's not talk about that," he coaxed, and his words worked their magic. I didn't want to think about it either.

He reached across and wrapped his fingers in mine, his touch warm and soft. He leaned over, his breath brushing my lips, waiting. I swayed forward when a loud clunk echoed outside. A very unnatural clunk considering we were on a boat and waves don't make loud thump-like noises.

Three

"WHAT'S THAT?" I WHISPERED, tightening my grip on Malcolm.

He motioned me to the side, lifted the seat of the bench to grab a pistol, then moved the curtains a fraction and peeked outside. "Stay here." He slipped through the door, quiet as an assassin.

My hands grew sweaty and my heart pounded. I leaned against the wall because my legs could barely hold me. I imagined the monks in dark robes surrounding the boat, or Will, Malcolm's brother, a step away from boarding, a sniper rifle or sharpened knife in hand. What if they'd already gotten to Malcolm? He could be splayed out on the dock, leaking blood into the sea from a knife to his side, while I sat here.

I crept toward the door.

Another loud thunk.

I stifled a scream. Biting down on the inside of my cheek, I nudged open the door with my foot and prayed the hinges were oiled. Thankfully, no creaks. The cooler night air seeped through the opening and sent goosebumps down my arms.

Instead of another clunk, I heard a scuffle of footsteps on the dock. The thuds of fists. Muted groans. I managed to inch forward and dared to poke my head out.

Malcolm wrestled on the docks with a man dressed in dark clothes. They jabbed and ducked. Their fight ebbed and flowed as they both tried to get in a good hit. If it weren't for the white of his eyes and the gleam of the knife, the attacker would be hard to see. I blinked. A knife? Nausea swept through me, and my legs almost gave way.

The attacker took Malcolm out with one swipe of his leg and then the knife was at his throat. With a maneuver that could only come from years of training, Malcolm grabbed the man's arm and twisted, knocking the long bladed knife across the docks. Only feet away from me.

Their bodies entwined. First one on top, then the other. The knife glistened on the docks, calling to me. The muffled sounds of the fight faded, and it was just me and the knife. I stepped onto the dock and inched forward with one eye on the fight. The attacker threw Malcolm against the dock, and his head dangled over the side. With one twist his neck could be broken. My hand snaked out and grabbed the handle of the knife.

"Enough!" I yelled, brandishing my weapon. Energy surged through me rippling through my limbs. My hand shook and the knife wavered.

Malcolm struggled and his legs twitched under the attacker's body. The man's hands were around Malcolm's throat.

"Stop!" I yelled, my voice rising to a scream.

The attacker stopped and turned back. He saw the knife and jumped to his feet. Malcolm scrambled up, breathing heavy, his hands massaging his neck. They were puppets and I was the one holding the strings. My arms strained under the weight of the rather large knife, but it created the desired effect. Malcolm moved toward me, but with one warning glance from the attacker, he stopped.

My arm dropped and the knife dangled, barely in my grip. Even without seeing his olive-skinned face, curly hair and chocolate eyes, I knew. Adamos, the monk I'd saved from the catacombs in Paris. But I couldn't have the people closest to me fighting.

When we first arrived in Greece, he'd refused to see any doctors or lodge any formal complaints about his hostage situation, so Mom and I spent the first couple months helping him recover. Okay, Mom did most of the work. I just hung out and distracted him with idle teen chatter. Slowly over the past months, he'd become my fast friend, my only confidant.

Adamos stepped toward me.

I whipped the knife back up, ready for action, so they'd take me seriously. My voice became a growl. "This stops here and now. I will not have you two killing each other off."

Malcolm stepped back, his right eyebrow raised. "You know this creep?"

I flashed him a wry grin. "The Greek bodyguard? Remember?"

"You were serious?" Malcolm asked, giving Adamos a sideways glance of suspicion mixed with a little bit of respect.

"I don't joke anymore, not when it comes to my life or the lives of my family and friends." I thought about Aimee safe with her grandfather, and safe from Malcolm's family.

Adamos moved a bit closer. "We need to talk."

"Whatever you have to say, you can say it in front of him." I held the knife higher.

Adamos hesitated, his eyes piercing through to the hidden part of me, the part I didn't show anyone but him lately. The faint light from Malcolm's boat outlined Adamos's face, his strong nose and set jaw. His head tilted in question and I wished I'd mentioned my crush on my mortal enemy before now. The three-way tension between all of us increased.

Finally, with stiff movements, Adamos bowed. "I will be watching." He gently loosened the knife from my grip and tucked it into his clothing. After flashing a warning look at Malcolm, he left the scene. Soon he was nothing but a flicker of a shadow and then he disappeared completely.

I sighed and swayed, my legs weak after the adrenaline rush of their fight. Malcolm strode over and guided me into his boat, his hand firm on my back.

"What were you thinking?" he asked, his voice tight with anger. With jerky movements, he pulled the curtain aside and peeked out.

I wiped hair from my face with a shaky hand. "You don't understand." Then any remaining walls between us came crashing down. "Adamos is the monk I saved in the catacombs. We've helped him recover. He's been my friend here in Greece when I knew no one. When I walk the streets, I know he has my back. His respect means a lot to me, and I think I just lost it." My voice wavered, on the verge of cracking. "He knows everything about our families."

"Fine." Malcolm sighed, the tension dissipating, then he pulled me into his arms. I breathed in the scent of his shirt: a combination of soap, sweat, and the night air woven together. We stayed like that and I tried to forget about everything else and just soak in that moment, with Malcolm back.

He murmured into my hair. "Let's run away."

I stiffened. "What?"

He spoke, his voice low, his face serious. "We could do it. You and me."

"No way." I took another step back. "That's crazy. I can't just leave. My mom's here and your family..." The trembling started in the tips of my fingers and slowly spread as the truth hit me like one big tidal wave crashing against shore, tearing up anything in its path. If Malcolm was in Greece, then his family was too. Which meant they knew where to find my mom and me. I had to get out of there, find Adamos and go back home. Maybe Mom would listen to me.

"Just hear me out." He grabbed my hand. "We could take off until this business with our families has been sorted out. I have ways of leaving so no one will know where we've gone. You'd be perfectly safe." His words were urgent, suggesting he'd thought about this before. "I could take care of everything. And you could still stay in touch with your mom."

I hesitated. Safe? I'd be perfectly safe? The thought of taking off with Malcolm was tempting, but I thought back to Paris and the times Malcolm had held back the truth. I didn't fully trust him. I shook my head no. My goal was to glue my family back together, not run. "I can't. You don't understand. Your family's presence in Greece is a direct threat to my life, and my mom's life. But I can't just run away."

Malcolm started to argue, but I held up my hand for him to stop. "I don't want to hear it." I strode past him to the door. "I've stayed way too long as it is."

He didn't try to convince me to stay as I left his boat, and as soon as I was far enough away, I fled into the night and back home. I hoped I hadn't made the biggest mistake of my life.

Four

THE NEXT DAY, SITTING at the coffee shop in the public gardens, Mom and I acted like absolutely nothing was wrong with our lives. I switched back and forth between studying the breakfast menu and tracing imaginary cracks in the table as she did most of the talking. Malcolm's plan to run away kept pulsing in the back of my mind, teasing me to change my decision. The fact that he wanted me to run away told me I was in danger, but I couldn't leave Mom.

Was Malcolm's family keeping an eye on us? Or did they have hired thugs? I'd never asked Malcolm about the specifics of the inner workings of their crime family, so I searched every person, invading their personal space with my eyes, looking for anything that might be a weapon, and studying their body language. Did they fidget? Or glance my way too often?

Mom drummed her fingers against the side of her teacup. "Would you like anything to eat? Are you hungry?"

"No, not at all," I said, attempting to keep my voice high and enthusiastic.

Okay so we never exactly chatted like old pals. We couldn't when she kept too many secrets. She'd evaded any questions about the spy thing going on with our family, insisting she'd been in Paris on a scrapbooking convention when she picked me up.

Whatever. Scrapbooking my ass.

Except now I had my own secrets. Malcolm and possibly the rest of his family, our mortal enemies, a brood of assassins, were in Greece. I definitely didn't plan on telling her about the constant fluttering in my chest since I'd seen him or my fantasies about running away and kissing him along the shore of the Caribbean, his soft lips pressed against mine.

She blew on her tea and steam swirled. I hugged my mug, clueless as to why she dragged me to the gardens. We'd already had "conversations" about Paris and how Malcolm's family had used a fake death threat on Jolie Pouffant—the magnificent pastry chef—to lure Mom out of hiding. But she'd shut down on the subject before the words were out of my mouth, which didn't leave much for us to talk about.

"So..." And that was all I could find to say.

"Have you been keeping up with any online classes?" Mom asked, glancing to the right and then at her watch.

"Um, sure," I mumbled, and then out of curiosity, I said, "Actually, I stopped the courses back in Paris."

"That's wonderful," she murmured and absently sipped her tea.

That was what I thought; she wasn't really paying attention. The awkward silence wedged between us and I moved on to people watching. A heavyset man strode toward us, dressed up in a tie and cravat with a fancy walking stick. Who dresses like that anymore? Was it a disguise? I gripped my coffee, hoping it was still hot enough to cause damage or make a distraction so I could get in a good kick.

"Marisa!" His voice boomed across the coffee shop startling a group of scavenger pigeons.

Mom shot up from the chair and smoothed her hair. "Constance, so glad you could meet us."

I almost snorted coffee through my nose. Constance? And Mom had invited him? She was sneakier than I thought.

He waved a hand. "Sorry to keep you waiting. Ready for a walk through the gardens?"

"Yes." Mom's voice was breathless. She turned to me. "This is my daughter, Savvy."

"Ah yes, Savvy. I've heard so much about you. Charmed." He stuck out his hand to shake but I ignored the gesture.

"Savvy," Mom said with warning in her voice, "Constance and I met the other week at a bird lovers meet-up.

"Birds?" Yeah, right. Mom had never loved birds. I narrowed my eyes and studied him. He appeared innocent enough with the hawk-like nose, the tiny bird pins on his vest, and the binoculars around his neck. Was Mom spying on him? Maybe protecting him from certain assassins we knew? Hmm. I'd have to keep an eye on the situation.

"Shall we?" Constance held his arm out to my mom and she slipped her arm through his like they were on a date.

We strolled through dirt paths in between flowering bushes, their red and yellow petals reflecting the bright sun and attracting the honeybees. Tall gangly palm trees offered little to no shade. We walked through a tunnel-like thing with flowers and plants growing on the framed wooden structure above us. We crossed a bridge over a manmade duck pond. Constance pointed out birds like the Eurasian Collared Dove, the Great Tit—I sniggered—and the short-toed Treecreepers. Mom acted enraptured by his whole spiel. I kept wishing Adamos would rescue me. Couldn't he see I was in mortal danger of being bored to death? Or maybe after last night, he'd given up on me.

"What about the Acropolis in Athens?" I asked. "That would be fun to check out sometime." I'd been here five months and hadn't seen it yet.

Constance raised his voice in exclamation over a Spotted Flycatcher, his hands waving in excitement like a toddler on the merry-go-round.

Every time I made a suggestion about where to go in the park—like the ancient ruins—Constance steered us in the opposite direction. Mom didn't seem to have much control over the outing either, which I was sure drove a control freak like her crazy.

I'd had enough. Maybe I was a control freak too. "I have to use the bathroom."

"Can it wait, honey?" Mom asked, not even looking at me but hanging on birdman's every word.

"Not really. I'm about to pee my pants. The coffee caught up to me."

Constance flashed me a look of complete disdain. Like talking about normal bodily functions was beneath him. Mom pulled out a map of the gardens. Immediately, birdman pulled it from her hands.

"I'll show you the restroom on our way past the duck pond. It's the best place to see the magpies." He didn't wait for my answer but hooked Mom's arm in his again and walked away.

"Actually," I spoke up, "I'm eighteen and a half and can manage to find the bathroom on my own. I'll catch up to you later."

But Constance had started up a constant stream of chatter and my voice went unheard. Mom laughed in a fake sort of way at what was most likely his lame bird jokes. Her laugh pierced what was left of my ability to put up with this jerk, so I left, quite pleased with my moment of rebellion. The bathrooms couldn't be that hard to find without a map.

One minute I was smiling, relishing my independence and the next thing I knew a blast deafened my ears. I flipped around to see a trashcan exploding. Right next to my mom.

Five

PIECES OF COFFEE CUPS, banana peels and diapers flew in every direction while debris and dust floated in the air. Most tourists scattered in opposite directions and other snapped pictures with their cell phones and caught live footage of the twisted pieces of plastic.

I rushed toward Mom, but Constance already had his arm around her, leading her away to safety. I followed and sat next to them on the bench, my legs shaking. A bomb? What were the chances of that happening? The spider prickles returned in full force and I swept the scene for anyone suspicious. Was this a random prank played by some rebellious teenager? Or was the bomb planted with someone hidden, waiting nearby, ready to press the button when Mom walked past it?

Mom patted Constance's arm. "Would you be so kind as to bring us some bottled water?"

"Absolutely," Constance affirmed. "I'll be back in a jiffy." Then he took off at a rapid pace, which I figured would soon leave him huffing and puffing.

As soon as Constance followed the path and was out of her sight, Mom changed from the withering, needy bomb victim to the confident, savvy spy. She snapped her fingers and Adamos appeared from between the nearby palm trees. Not sure how he managed to pull that off.

"Take Savvy home," she instructed.

"What?" I cried. "No way. I'm not leaving you here."

Mom grasped my hand. "It's too dangerous. Adamos will make sure you're safe at home."

I yanked my hand away and crossed my arms, refusing to move from the bench. "Something's going on and I want to help."

Mom pressed her lips together and doubts flickered across her face. If only she'd let me in and tell me what was going on with Constance: if she truly had fallen in love with bird watching or if he'd been targeted by a certain family we knew.

Mom's voice wavered. "You really want to know the truth?"

Adamos nodded his approval as if he could hear the debate raging in her head and thought she could trust me.

"Yes!" I scooted closer and leaned forward. "I'm ready for anything. Count me in as part of the team." I imagined she and I working together, diffusing bombs, flying through the air and saving each other's lives while James Bond music played.

Mom narrowed her eyes. "I have strong reason to believe that Will and his family have targeted Constance. I'll give you one chance on an easy mission but one that will be a tremendous help. First, go home and get something to eat. You'll need nourishment. Then keep an eye on Constance's house for the evening and record any suspicious activity. Adamos knows where he lives and will accompany you."

"Seriously?" My excitement deflated. "That's it?"

Mom lifted my chin with her finger. "We start small and build from there. Okay?"

"Fine," I grumbled but on the inside I was bursting with excitement. This first mission, this small assignment, could be the start of something much bigger. As in earning my mom's trust and putting my family back together.

The next hour or so was one big blur. Back at home in the small adobe house Mom had rented, Adamos led me to the fire pit out back. Then he disappeared back inside. The scattered ashes in between the large rocks swayed in the wind until a stronger breeze picked up the gray fluff and carried it away. In these small moments, quiet times when I had a chance to reflect, I couldn't help but think of Dad. He'd want to be in on this too but Mom had already stated with great emphasis that she didn't want to drag him into danger. Here was my chance to find some control and question Adamos about Mom.

"Hey!" I called out. "Are you in there?"

"Yes, yes, I'm here. Sorry to worry you." He placed a tray with a white box on it on the small patio table then sat in the chair next to me.

I focused on the box, my curiosity piquing. Clear wax paper poked out the sides, the kind of wax paper used to separate certain foods, like pastries. Was that dried glaze on the side?

Adamos handed me a glass of water. "Your father is fine. I have someone looking out for him."

He always seemed to know my thoughts. My throat closed up a bit. I even missed Dad's burnt mac and cheese and his off key version of Barry Manilow.

Adamos placed his hand over his heart. "We carry the people we love here." He thumped his chest. "They are always with us even if we can't look in their eyes, hear their voice, or hold their hand."

He clasped his hands together and stopped talking but it was too late. The emotion crackled in his words and the mist pooled in his eyes. He had a past. He knew heartbreak, and I had a feeling it was a lot worse than mine.

"I'm sorry," I said, wishing I could take away his pain even if I couldn't understand it. It didn't seem the right time to ask about Mom's spy life or why the two of them seemed to have a history I knew nothing about. At the same time, I didn't often have Adamos so close and vulnerable. "How did you and my mom meet?"

"Ah. That is not my story to tell. I'm afraid you'll have to wait on your mother for that one. Let's just say, we've known each other for several years, before Paris."

He nodded, indicating that was all he'd share. We sat in silence, both reliving our memories. Finally he found his words and his fingers found the edge of the white box. The wax paper crinkled, the noise evoking memories of my past life with French pastries.

"Any troubles in my life brought me to you, to my real purpose in life, to protect you. But I had to travel the tough roads to get here."

"Do you have any regrets?" Of course he did. Following around a teenage girl?

He lifted the lid of the box and the smell of cinnamon wafted up. "That is the wrong question and only leads to trouble."

I tried again, my eyes darting from the box to his face and back to the box. "You really believe in all that fate stuff?"

"I didn't at first." He closed the box and pulled my hand into his. "Not too many years ago I lost my sister. She was your age." His voice clouded with emotion. "You remind me of her, your dark hair and eyes."

"I'm so sorry."

I studied his olive skin, chocolate eyes, and the way his dark hair curled over his ears. He was maybe five years older than me? My heart wrenched. He lost his sister and got me in return? How could I ever live up to a memory?

"Never refuse a gift or feel guilty for it. You saved my life in Paris. Let me help you."

"Will I ever know the truth about my mom's past?" I blurted. "Will she ever tell me?"

"Be patient with your mother," he said. "Everything she does is for you, for your safety. Even when her choices are a puzzle, remember you're not seeing the entire picture. Be happy for what she has offered, not what she hasn't." He opened the box all the way and pulled aside the wax paper. "As soon as you've finished and have cleaned up, we'll be ready to go."

I sat, unmoving, wide-eyed, taking in the sight of the apple turnover topped with a clear gaze dotted with cinnamon and dripping off the sides in chunks. I closed my eyes and cherished every bite like a monk does his nightly prayers. The mixed flavors of apple, cinnamon and sugar melted in my mouth. It disappeared fast and sitting alone, with the taste of turnover still on my tongue, the truth hit me. No more watching boring tourists in the market place or twiddling my thumbs in my bedroom. I leaned over and put my head between my knees and puffed in and out as a terrified thrill rose in my chest.

My first mission.

Half an hour later, Adamos motioned to follow him through the gardens, until we found the perfect spot to view the house between a rhododendron bush and a bust of a naked woman, just outside the reach of any outside lights if they were to flick on suddenly. We crouched in the shrubbery, deep in the garden, close enough to observe, but far enough away not to be seen. Landscaped bushes surrounded the house like a moat. Grape vines crawled and twisted along a wooden overhang, and paved walkways wound through gardens littered with statues. The last of the setting sun painted the sky in glorious colors of pink and orange and shadowed the garden creating this incredibly romantic atmosphere.

In other words, nothing suspicious.

As I surveyed the house, and searched for any kind of disturbance, the upper story windows seemed to wink at me as if they were all in on some kind of silent joke. Was Mom just keeping me busy? The pristine white washed walls were crawling with ivy, and perfectly pruned hedges lined the outside of an outdoor patio. Maybe that was why Malcolm's family was out to get him. Maybe with laundered money, Constance supported the wrong cause that could set off a global crisis or something.

With Adamos right next to me, I kneeled with one foot up, ready to sprint back through the gardens if there was a sign of anyone or anything. But slowly, as the minutes passed, my excitement waned, as we sat and sat and sat. I chased away a cricket and watched a large spider spin her web, and I built a temple of small pebbles from the walkway.

Every time I asked Adamos a question, he put a finger to his lips and pointed at the house. So I sat and sat and sat while studying the house and gardens for any signs of Malcolm's family. A chip of paint might've fallen off the window trim. A bird—possibly the Great Tit—flew into a birdhouse, and the petals of small red flowers on the trellis moved in the breeze.

Nothing spectacular until a dark shadow flickered to the left of me. When I whipped my head around to get a better look, it was gone. I imagined the lean form of an intruder moving with stealth upon the unsuspecting house.

My mission just made a one eighty turn.

Six

"HEY!" I HISSED. "Did you see that?"

Adamos shook his head no and motioned to keep watching. I bit my lip and studied the dark places, the hidden spots. Anywhere intruders would most likely be. Seconds passed and I saw nothing. I sighed, about to accept that I'd imagined it, my desperation for excitement reaching new pathetic levels, when the figure approached a window and seconds later jimmied the lock and entered the house.

I gasped and with a flailing of my arms tried to get Adamos's attention, but he remained calm, sitting cross-legged with his hands folded under his chin in a very meditative position. Finally I was able to speak.

"There!" I pointed. "Did you see that?"

He pointed to my knapsack. "Observe and record but do not take action."

I was a spy. I could not sit on my lazy butt and twiddle my thumbs. I studied the house, the hard angles of the roof and the turret windows, and imagined the man sliding across floors, entering and unlocking safes. What if Constance owned valuable jewels? Or what if he stowed his entire life savings under his mattress and it was all he had to his name?

This one robbery could put him out on the street and then Mom would ask why I hadn't done something to stop it. She'd say it takes instinct to know when to break the rules and she'd shake her head and refuse to work with me. My instinct came in the form of a burning sensation in my heart and an itch in my feet, urging me to follow him.

"We've got to go and see what he's doing. Take pictures! Observe." I added in some more enthusiastic arm gestures to convince him. "I promise I won't do anything. I'll watch and take pictures with my trusty phone, then I'll report back here."

He narrowed his eyes.

I pulled out the only ammo I had left. "Mom sent me here expecting absolutely nothing to happen. We'd sit here. I'd get bored and then stop bugging her. If she learns someone broke in and we did nothing? She'll be furious." I flashed him a sly smile. "But, if I chase away the intruder, I might earn her trust. Right?"

He pursed his lips and gazed at the house. Finally he nodded. "Do what you must to get a closer look while staying hidden. Then return back here. I'll be watching."

After almost knocking Adamos over with a giant hug, I sprinted through the gardens until I reached the house. I pressed my back to the outside wall to catch my breath. Then I heard the tinkling high pitch of my mom's fake laughter probably at Constance cracking lame bird jokes. The front door opened and shut. They were inside. Mom's arrival changed everything. I had no choice but to enter. I would approach with the expertise of a professional spy. Mom's safety and the wellbeing of her companion were at stake. They'd need someone on the inside. They needed me.

With my fingers under the top of window, I tugged to see if it was still unlocked. It lifted no problem and I was inside. My first official break-in in Greece, and it felt good. Okay, I won't mention the long and painful scrape across my stomach when I gracefully wormed my way in, or the scratches on my leg when I used one of the perfectly pruned bushes as a footstool.

The shadows became my friends and I snaked through hallways and up the stairs as if I were invisible. My feet were so light on the ground I was more like a butterfly. That could be my future code name: The Butterfly. Sounded rather intimidating in an ironic sort of way. My mom laughed a few rooms away so I crept in the opposite direction through a humongous room that must be for grand parties.

The mutterings of a thief echoed from the upstairs, as he possibly plundered jewels or stacks of money. My heart skipped a few beats. After scaling the stairs, I grabbed a porcelain vase off a side table and crept toward the room at the end of the hall.

I stopped and listened but the desire to catch a glimpse of the intruder's face pushed me forward, inch by inch, until I peeked around the corner.

Most of the room lay in darkness, but the guy's flashlight flicked back and forth on the desk, revealing opened drawers that took on the appearance of a row of crooked teeth. Papers were scattered on the floor, the chair, the desk. My instinct went into full non-stop action.

With the vase lifted above my head, I burst into the room and aimed for the intruder. I brought my arms down and broke the vase on what I thought was the man's head, with only the slightest tickle of guilt in the back of my mind for the vase. The man ducked out of the way and the vase cracked against the hard corners of a desk instead of the soft skull of a man's head.

Ugly squawking and shrill whistles of warning blasted my ears and I stumbled back at the sudden onslaught of noise. I searched the room, seeing the flash of metal bird cages, but before I could get a look at the guy's face, his hands landed on my chest and he shoved me to the floor.

"You bitch," he said, his ugly tone of voice sending creepy shivers through my body.

And then he ran.

"What?" I muttered. "Afraid of a teenage girl?"

Minutes passed as I picked my way through the pottery shards. I wondered if I could brush them under a rug. While I was in the middle of scooping the pieces up with a magazine to dump them into a desk drawer, footsteps thundered in the hallway. Seconds later, Mom, Constance, and Adamos turned on the light and crashed into the room. I cringed at the scattered mess, very aware of my somewhat failed mission. I'd wanted to play the role of glorious victor and have the guy bound and gagged on the floor with my foot on top of him.

Constance dropped to his knees and tried to puzzle some of the shards together. "Oh, my Ming vase!"

But his attention didn't stay on the broken vase as the birds continued their loud complaints at the bright light and commotion. His hands flew to his cheeks in horror as he rushed from cage to cage throughout the room, mumbling words of solace. I hadn't dared look at Mom yet, but I didn't need to. I could feel her disapproving glare drilling through me. I sensed a very long lecture in my near future.

"My poor babies." Constance fluttered his hands by his sides as if he were a bird himself. "Please! Please, leave, all of you. I must calm them down." He immediately started cooing and handing out tidbits of birdseed.

Mom grabbed my arm, yanked me to my feet and led me out into the hallway. Her rage was palpable in her tone of voice and the fact that my fingers were going numb from her grip. "What happened to just observing and recording?"

"I was observing on the inside because an intruder had sneaked past us in the garden and entered the house. Like any good spy, I followed my instinct to save whatever treasures were stored in the house. And to protect you." My words trailed off and I realized how amateurish I sounded in the wake of the catastrophe. "At least I chased off the intruder."

She pulled Adamos to the side, their muttered conversation low enough so I couldn't hear. She faced me, her lips pressed together in grim determination and I saw my chances, my hopes, my dream of working with her fade away.

"Return home with Adamos, and I'll see if Constance will even let me near him again. This whole mission could be compromised." She turned and strode back to birdman.

"But, um, we're still a team, right?" I asked.

She whipped around at the doorway. "Team members follow directions, and you did not."

I'd failed. Completely and utterly failed.

I wandered the streets, Adamos following in the shadows. My feet followed the natural path they always found and led me to the shoreline. In no certain words, I'd told Adamos that I'd needed some air before we went home. I wasn't happy with my spoiled brat moment but my whole life had fallen into pieces on my first real mission. The rocky sand shifted under my feet and I found a spot to plop down and feel sorry for myself.

The waves licked the rocks and a cool breeze whipped off the sea. I shivered and rubbed my arms. The sun had disappeared completely. I grabbed a nearby stick and dug at the sand, something, anything not to think about my life. Both Mom and Adamos wanted to keep me safe. That was the justification behind all their decisions. On the wake of this last disaster, I could never talk with Mom about Malcolm. Kissing him and succumbing to his charms—and his lips— was like playing with the devil. At any time the heat could turn dangerous. Was his family connected to the break in at Constance's house? Maybe they were looking for hard, cold facts before slitting his throat over a bowl of granola.

I was so consumed in and enjoying my pity party, that I didn't even hear the footsteps behind me. So when a hand touched my shoulder, I screamed and jumped away.

Seven

"HOLY CRAP! WAY TO sneak up on a girl." Then I was thankful the night hid my blush. Of course, he was nearby.

I expected a lecture, or one of his famous riddles, but instead Adamos dropped a stack of kindling in front of me. He piled the pieces of wood up in a circle of bigger rocks and within minutes a fire warmed me. His silence wasn't abnormal. I mean the guy wasn't much of a social butterfly. Darkness shadowed his face so I couldn't even tell what he was thinking. He'd want to know why I'd fraternized with the enemy. I could explain about Malcolm and the connection we formed in Paris. I could tell him that Malcolm had plans. My heart fluttered. Or I could tell him I didn't realize how strong my feelings were for Malcolm until I saw him again.

When he spoke, his voice cut through the dark.

"There is much we do not know for I left the brethren and the monastery too early, before learning the whole truth." He poked at the fire and I wasn't sure if he was talking more to himself or me. "If I'd known that pulling your mother from the ocean that day would mean my life would change forever I would've dug around for the truth a little earlier."

Holy moly—hold the phone. He slipped. He totally slipped. He pulled Mom from the ocean? "Say that again?"

A smile carved his face and I knew he wouldn't leak any more secrets.

"The whole time in Paris is dark for me," he said. "I remember talking to you but I can't recall the details of my abduction."

I tucked my knees close to my chest. "To tell you the truth, I've been trying to forget the whole experience."

"Do you remember anything?" he prodded.

His words were soft, but they did the job and brought the memories to the surface. My experience in the catacombs of Paris might be a blur, but certain conversations were branded into my brain forever. I couldn't help but glance right and left into the darkness, trying to see an invisible enemy.

"Something about monks trying to kill off my family and Malcolm's," I said, studying the fire. The flames constantly morphed but stayed the same too, consuming the air, out of control but in control at the same time.

"Yes. Monks I once respected and called brothers." He gazed across the Mediterranean. "I'm afraid we'll never know the full mystery behind their actions."

I followed his gaze. "Yeah, but they're holed away up on some mountaintop, right?"

He pointed across the sea. "They are on an island not too far from here. That is why I've been so protective and wish your Mom would move you to another country. Anywhere but here in Greece."

Crap. It was worse than I thought. My imagined fears weren't so imaginary. "She'll never leave her new "mission" A.K.A operation save birdman."

The words left a bitter taste in my mouth, but it was the truth. Mom loved me. I knew that. But she'd become a mystery with most of her focus on her current mission. As we sat, both lost in our thoughts of regret, the flames slowly withered and died.

"There are certain precautions you can take to protect yourself."

He didn't have to say anymore. I knew exactly whom he referred to. "But you don't understand—"

"That might be true but I fear this boy will never be able to leave his roots, his family, or who he's been molded to be. He might've spared your life once but there's no guarantee that any notions of romance will save your life the second time."

There it was. The hard cold truth. Pressure built in my chest, the argument hot on my tongue. I wanted to blurt out that he was wrong, that Malcolm had a plan for us, but the last of the fire spit out its warmth and just coals remained. The dark swallowed any remaining light. Adamos seemed deep in thought, battling something inside.

"What? Go ahead you might as well say whatever it is you're thinking."

He smiled, but it quickly disappeared. "We should not stay in Greece much longer."

"What do you mean? Leave?" The moment Mom took on another mission, any option to leave Greece behind was snuffed out. I scoffed silently. "Good luck with that." It would never happen. Mom would never leave. And I wouldn't leave either.

"I've been keeping tabs on the family, especially the other brother." Adamos threw sand on the remaining coals. "It might not be safe anymore. I'll talk to your mother."

An idea sparked and grew at a tremendous pace and I knew I wouldn't run away with Malcolm. Not yet. Mom might not let me help her protect Constance but I could still do my part, behind the scenes. I was brilliant. "You've been keeping tabs on Malcolm's family?"

"Yes." Adamos nodded.

"So, purely hypothetically, of course, you could tell me where Malcolm's brother might be at any particular time during the day?"

Adamos's eyes glittered in the dark. "Why yes, I could. But purely hypothetically, why would you want to know?"

"Um." I stumbled over my words. Adamos wasn't always a rule follower. The other night, he'd let me approach Constance's house, knowing full well I might enter. Just maybe, he'd give me some wiggle room on this. "Well, purely hypothetically, maybe someone with a bit of spying under her belt should keep an eye on the older brother. Someone young and kinda cute." I flipped my hair. "Someone who knows the family, knows their real business. Someone who can flirt with the older brother and possibly learn their secret plans for one Constance Gerald, on the sly."

"Absolutely not!" Adamos stated with a bit of steel behind his words.

I refused to quit. "If this someone were to be successful then she and her mom could leave the country where they currently reside and find a nice, quiet place tucked away in the country."

"No," he said, with less conviction.

"This someone would stay in public and would have her secret bodyguard watching at all times." I held my breath, praying he'd see the wisdom in my plans. "Perfectly safe."

Adamos narrowed his eyes and stared through to the very heart of me. A battle raged in the way he clenched his jaw and tensed his shoulders. Finally, he spoke quietly as if passing on top secret information. "Malcolm's grandmother visits the market three times a week and she always buys fresh lemons. His mother and father diligently attend social functions, and his older brother runs on the beach almost every morning."

"Almost every morning?" I repeated, a devious and dangerous plan forming.

"Hypothetically, yes."

"Hope I don't run into them," I said, then laughed it off. "Like that would ever happen."

"And Savvy?" he said. "Hypothetically, I'll be watching you."

Eight

THE NEXT FEW MORNINGS at the crack of dawn I pounded the pavement. I sucked it up and pushed through my intense pain and strong dislike of elevating my heart rate. The best part was ending my run at the beach, the cool breeze drying my sweat and the feeling of being the only person in the world.

On the fourth morning, I wiggled my butt into the sand and studied the rhythm of the waves rushing up on the shore and then receding. My thoughts were rudely interrupted by a ferocious growling. Slobber splashed my arm and oozed down my cheek. A creature so large I thought a prehistoric dinosaur still existed breathed on me, with a stink so horrid I almost passed out. I tried to roll away but couldn't. Thoughts of death by a trained dog flitted through my brain.

A whistle sounded and then a harsh voice. "Down, Prince."

Slowly, the spit and dog breath were pulled off me and I gawked at the humongous Great Dane. Holy cow it was

49

gargantuan. Ginormous. Then I was drawn to the gorgeous man in front of me and my jaw dropped a bit further. Board shorts, ripped tee and a faded hat completed the image of a carefree young man. His wind-blown hair flopped across his forehead, and his strong jaw line led to chapped lips. His eyes held flecks of charcoal, just like Malcolm, and his smile crooked up on one side making it more like a smirk.

Finally, my days of running had paid off. Exactly whom I'd been waiting for. Will, Malcolm's older brother. He undoubtedly knew who I was and I could never forget the guy who shot a bullet into my leg in Paris. Let the games begin.

"Hi there." He waved while holding back Prince. "Sorry about that. Normally no one's here this time of day and I like to give him a little freedom." He rubbed the dog's ears and cooed. "Isn't that right, Prince? That's right. You like to run, don't ya boy?"

All at once I was impressed with his cleverness. Not only was Will handsome in a classic movie star way but he was an even better actor and talented master of disguises than Malcolm. From what I knew, Will was anything but carefree, more like a meticulously trained assassin who left no room for accidents, including meeting me at the beach.

Will plunked down in the sand. "Sit, Prince."

Prince growled at me and bared his teeth as if he knew our families were mortal enemies.

"I don't think he likes me very much." I wasn't usually scared of dogs, but Prince was like a monster from a Greek myth.

"Ah, he's a big puppy. Just protective of his family." Will pointed and commanded Prince to sit again. The monster dog obeyed.

"So," I willed up my most confident, savvy tone of voice, "fancy meeting another American here."

"No kidding." With a casual flip of the head, he revealed his eyes. "I love traveling and exploring foreign cities but it's nice to meet someone who likes Pizza Hut and baseball stadium hotdogs." He narrowed his eyes. "You do like pizza, don't you?"

I huffed. "Of course." I stared suspiciously back. "The real question is do you like the meat lovers pizza with everything on it, because I can't be talking with you if you don't."

"You're in luck." He winked and smiled in the most charming manner that would have most girls swooning and fanning their bodies from overheating.

I pulled back, a little shocked. Was I flirting? With the enemy? The most disturbing fact was that it came so easily with Will. Not sure what I'd expected. A slimy poser who wouldn't know how to relate to people? Certainly not this very real, very cute guy. I knew he wasn't a teen. Malcolm was eighteen. Will had to be at least twenty.

"What brought you to Greece?" he asked after throwing a tennis ball for Prince.

"Um," I stumbled over what to say. Yes, I'd planned this meeting, but I hadn't fully prepared for when it actually happened. "Birds," I blurted out.

He raised an eyebrow. "Birds, huh."

"Um, yeah. Mom's a fanatic and we're here to sightsee. That's right. We've saved up for years just to see, um," I searched for one of the birds Constance had pointed out. "The, um, the Great Tit."

I almost asked Will to just assassinate me right then and there. Seriously? What about the magpie? Something that didn't include a female body part.

Will smirked. "They certainly are fantastic. Love them myself."

Total perv. Even if I'd asked for it. I stared out at the sea and the first sailboats to cross the expanse, their white sails flashing and laughing at me in the morning sun. I was quite certain I looked like a lobster. Time to redirect. "Why are you in Greece?" Other than to spy on my family and do a little assassinating, of course. "Vacationing?"

"Not birds, even though the Great Tit is a terrific reason. I'm here with family for a little bit of everything. Work. Play." Prince returned and dropped the ball at his feet. Will threw it again, his arm muscles rippling. "And everything in between."

At least he was honest and his deadpan teasing made him that much cuter. "Oh, what kind of work?"

"Boring family business type things. I'd put you to sleep if I got into it."

His words held a tiny hint of sarcasm because he and I both knew we were just playing a game, that really, I knew he was an assassin and he knew I was a spy.

Prince dropped the tennis ball at his feet and started running. I grabbed the ball. "May I?"

Will waved me on and I threw the ball as far as I could. Prince bounded down the beach, sand flying up behind him. Over the last few days, my attempt to brainwash myself must have seeped into my soul because I seemed to be naturally doing the spy thing, making myself approachable and vulnerable, being friendly, getting to know Will. This felt safe. Safer than walking through the market place, wondering when I'd feel a knife in my back. Keep your enemies close. That was my new mantra.

Prince ate up the distance on the way back, weaving around a group of women out to walk, and dropped the slimy ball at my feet. I laughed. And getting in with the family guard dog was a major bonus.

"You might be wondering why I came looking for you." Nerves caused my voice to crack the tiniest bit but I didn't think he noticed.

His face lost the light and flirty look and he stared as if trying to penetrate my brain and read my thoughts. "I was curious why you'd put yourself in danger," he spread his arms to include the empty shoreline, "at an almost-deserted beach where I could kill you in about two seconds with a quick snap of your neck."

I swallowed and almost choked on my spit. Words deserted me and my naive feeling of safety splintered.

"Don't worry. You're safe for now." Will stood and brushed the sand off his shorts, a smirk tugging on his lips. "How about pizza tonight?"

"Um, yeah?" My confidence slipped. I'd expected a bit more friction with my plan to infiltrate his life. Yet, he'd asked me out on a date after explaining how he could kill me. But a date could lead to another date, and another; and then, possibly, an invitation to his home. Later, under the cover of night, I could break in and search for their secret plans. Then presto—Constance would be safe, and Mom and I could contact Dad and be a family again. Fool proof.

"I know this terrific place. You have to try Greek pizza. It's incredible." The rising sun painted his skin with a warm glow, and his eyes radiated a look that said, Trust me. "That is if you have time in between bird watching." He flashed a predatory grin.

"Sure." I shivered a moment at the reality of setting a date with the enemy. "Why don't we meet someplace, then?"

"I know where you live. I'll whistle outside your house, so be listening." Then he leaned forward, a dangerous glint in his eye. "My little brother might get jealous. Are you sure you want to do this, Savvy?"

This was it. He was offering me a chance to stop this crazy scheme. I could back out and pretend I never talked to him. I opened my mouth to say the words, but then I thought about Mom lying, refusing to talk to me; and her dates with Constance, leaving me alone. "Yes, I'm sure." Then I leaned forward and added confidence to my words. "Are you sure you want to do this, Will?"

He smiled. "I look forward to it."

I had to figure out what to wear.

My closet overflowed with a pathetic assortment of clothes. I needed something that would give the clear message that I was someone to be feared. I ran my fingers through my shirts. Not the red top with sequins or the blue sleeveless. Both were way too snazzy. I whipped out a white button-up shirt and black jeans. They'd have to do.

"Savvy?" Mom called from her bedroom. She didn't have to call too loud because our walls were paper thin and right next to each other. "Someone's at the door. Could you get it?"

Oh, crap. Oh, crap. I did the last button of my shirt. What if Will came to the door? I hadn't brushed my hair or expertly applied lip gloss yet. I fluffed my hair for extra body then rushed and opened the door with a breathless, "What are you doing here?"

"Why, Savvy. I'd think your mom would've alerted you to the fact I was arriving for dinner per her invitation." Constance brushed past me and into our tiny abode, the smell of his aftershave cloying and obnoxious. It screamed slime ball. He was like the blob, rolling into our place, glomming onto everything and leaving behind a distinct layer of sticky ooze.

After a quick glance into the darkening streets, I didn't see a sign of Will, thankfully. I shut the door and whirled around. Mom's dinner date was the perfect excuse for me to leave. She flounced into our small living room, her skirt swirling around her legs. She had her hair up in some ridiculous hairdo and plastic beads around her neck.

"Constance, so glad you could make it." She batted her eyelashes.

I strolled back toward my room. "After I finish getting ready, I thought I'd hit the town tonight and do some shopping."

Mom trilled this ridiculous high-pitched giggle. "Don't be ridiculous, Savvy. We have company and I've prepared a special dish. Fresh Salmon steaks."

I hesitated at the edge of the hallway. So that was the way it was going to be? I got stir fry with mushy veggies and birdman gets Salmon? "Well, no one ever informed me, and I made plans," I stated rather firmly.

Mom poured the Blob a glass of wine, which he swirled like an expert and sniffed with his hawk nose. I swear he cast me a haughty glance when Mom wasn't looking.

Her voice lost its light tone. "No, Savvy. You'll be dining with us tonight and then staying inside."

I smothered the anger rising like a strong rip current. Constance smirked, a big cheesy grin on his face, but before he could speak, I stated, "I'm going to my room."

I sank onto the bed, my bravado fading, wanting, wishing for Dad, for Mom, for us to hit rewind and go back in time before everything got messed up. A slight knock at my window startled me and my back stiffened. I crawled across the bed and peered through the window.

Malcolm.

Nine

I LIFTED THE WINDOW A CRACK.

"You scared the crap out of me!" My words rushed out, laden with the stress from the evening. "You can't be here...my mom..." I didn't even need to ask how he and Will happened to know where I lived. It came with their line of work.

"Whoa. Sorry. Did you want me to use the front door?" He pushed the window up the rest of the way and leaned his elbows on the sill. His sly grin teased me and I couldn't help notice his resemblance to Will.

"No." I sank to my knees, drinking in the sight of him. I wanted to trace my fingers down his cheek and press my lips to his. But I couldn't, not with the secrets digging at my conscience. I mean my date with Will meant nothing, but I doubt Malcolm would see it that way.

Damn. Will would arrive any minute, and Mom would expect me at the table. "Not good timing."

"Come with me to the boat. We can talk further about...you know. Our plans." He leaned farther over the sill and curled a strand of my hair around his finger.

"Savvy?" Mom called out.

"I've got to go!" I tried to pull away but he wouldn't let me. "We'll talk later. Wait up for me." Then I slammed the window down. Why couldn't life be easy for once?

The door opened.

"What are you doing?" Mom demanded, standing in the doorway like my jail warden.

"Just catching some fresh air." The lie slipped out easily.

"I expect you at the table sooner than later." She turned to go.

"Mom?"

"What?" Her voice tightened as if she knew what I was going to ask.

"Stop sheltering me like I'm some sort of child." She didn't move so I continued. "Tell me everything and let me work with you. I promise I'll follow directions."

"Savvy." Her voice was condescending and tinted with frustration. Her back stiffened and a slight shudder passed through her body probably at the idea of an honest conversation. Clearly that scared the crap out of her. My question was answered. Any desire to press her for the truth drained away.

"Never mind. But I'm not coming to dinner. I feel kinda sick," I said.

"Fine. Get some rest." She left without another word.

Working with her to protect Constance was not an option. I slipped out the window, praying Malcolm was long gone, and let the cool evening air wash over me. My fresh start.

Out front, someone whistled the high notes of some obnoxious merry tune. I ran to the front of the house and intercepted Will. He stepped back and studied me, his arms crossed and his left eyebrow slightly raised.

"Hmm. Someone needs a night on the town."

"Let's go. Don't ask," I muttered.

He hooked his arm into mine and led me to his compact car. Nothing flashy like I expected. "I thought we could go into the city for the evening."

"Athens?" I'd lived here for almost half a year and had yet to visit this city.

"That okay?" he asked.

"No problem."

On the drive into the city, we didn't say a word. I tried, several times, to start up some banter or witty conversation with Will, but my heart wasn't in it. I'd left it back in my room, where Mom had shot me down. When I left Paris with her I'd hoped for a better life, a safer life. More importantly, an informed life. I wanted coffee talks and board games. I wanted field trips to the off-grid spots in Greece that typical tourists wouldn't know about it, but that Mom had researched. We'd spend time together, catching up on the past few years and forgiving. Instead I was left with the options of either taking action or wilting away in my bedroom while Mom dated Constance.

I sensed Will's perusal when he outright studied me every few minutes as if he was trying to read my thoughts and know my heart, my intentions.

"I'm not blind. I know you're looking at me," I said.

My voice was flat and lifeless. I wasn't here to flirt, not in the true sense of the word when it came to a boy and a girl. And not with the guy who'd shot me in the leg last year. But I had to bury the feelings of outrage and the desire for revenge, for now.

"Just gauging what kind of restaurant you might like tonight. And I know just the place."

"Fantastic," I said, without a trace of sarcasm.

I needed to turn off my emotions and become Savvy the Spy, the one who lives the cover of a happy, well-adjusted young woman, the one who lures the enemy in with honest lies and then cracks open the wealth of knowledge in his head and steals slivers of information. Without him knowing, of course.

We parked on the outskirts of the city. I stepped outside and the air felt different. No cool sea breeze or smell of salt. He led the way. Right on a narrow street, then left, then right, then straight. The sights and the sounds blurred around me into a jumble of colors and emotions: the hazy lights, the laughter of couples in love, and the strains of guitars and singing. I wanted that. Happiness. Peace. Fun. But those concepts seemed as foreign to me as the city streets beneath my feet.

"Hey, we're here." Will gently tugged on my arm.

"What?" I glanced at the adorable little restaurant in front of us. I couldn't even begin to pronounce the name, but I instantly fell in love with the outdoor patio, the red geraniums in potted holders along the deck, the simple white tables and wooden chairs. Nothing fancy but very welcoming. "Wow."

Will smiled for maybe the second time. "I knew it."

"Knew what?" I sneaked a sideways glance at him.

"That this would cheer you up. It might not be pizza but no one can stay sad for long in this place. Just wait and see."

Sad? I forced a smile and reprimanded myself about playing the role. "What're you talking about?"

"I'm pretty smart and can read people well. It's a gift. It's what makes me good at my job." He paused in front of the menu written on a whiteboard and read over the items.

"Don't worry. I'm not going to offer a therapy or handholding session. I'm not that kind of guy. We're here on business, right?"

I coughed, hiding my surprise at his candor. "Right."

We walked up the stairs and he ushered me to a table on the deck. About one minute after we sat and I struggled to say something impressive, two male waiters each with a white apron tied at the waist approached with a humongous tray filled with a gazillion plates of hot meals. Talk about service. Mom didn't know what she was missing just eating salads and stir-fry. Will pointed out the dishes with names like Fried Brinjals, Taskonikes, and Saganaki Cheese.

I shrugged and motioned for Will to order first. I went with a safe chicken dish with feta cheese, spinach and olives. And then we were eating. Just like that.

"Fast service," I offered up for conversation as I played with the napkin in my lap, twisting it into a rope.

"Yes, but I'd wait longer for this food." He picked up his fork and ate with a refined style, the way he sat straight and plucked carrot slivers off his plate, like he belonged at a grand party.

I pushed my chicken around, not in the mood to eat and slightly paranoid about getting a piece of spinach stuck between my teeth. The gap seemed to be widening between us. The fun and easy chatter we managed at the shore that morning disappeared. Why was I even considering cozying up to Will? It wouldn't work. He was too talented, too observant. My short stint as a spy in Paris had obviously been a fluke. I floundered through the rest of the meal with bits and pieces of random trivia and half-started conversations.

"I've got an idea," Will said, and finished up his last bite. "Let's get out of here. Obviously my advanced sense of reading people was off tonight. This place was supposed to cheer you up." He rubbed his chin and studied me. "We'll try something else." He dumped a bunch of bills on the table, stood, and offered his arm as if I was royalty.

He bought us hot drinks in to-go cups, and we trekked up the hill toward the Parthenon, past old churches and the ancient Supreme Court, then climbed stone-cut stairs. I shivered a bit after a few couples passed us. Would we be alone?

Small animals rustled in the landscaping, chasing after prey. The warning hoot of an owl pierced the night and echoed through the trees. Every few seconds, I peered into the shadows, hoping to see a flicker of movement, signaling that Adamos was nearby. I rubbed the goosebumps from my arm.

He wouldn't let anything happen to me.

Ten

FINALLY, WE STOOD AT the Acropolis overlooking the city. I tried to hide the sheen of sweat on my forehead from the climb, and I ignored the ache in my calf muscles. The giant pillars of the Parthenon towered behind us, and wild flowers pushed through every crack and crevice at our feet. In the distance, the moon hovered over the distant Mediterranean waters and lights twinkled from restaurants and homes, almost as if mocking me with their dimpled smiles. Was I a fool?

Will tapped my shoulder with his trigger finger. "Is this better?"

"It's lovely." I shivered at his light touch and sipped my latte, soaking in the silence that evening brought to such a tourist attraction. Clean air, untouched by the cooking smells wafting up from restaurants, washed over me with the breeze. I sighed. In that brief moment, peace swirled, holding me in her gracious arms. She stroked my hair, massaged my shoulders, and whispered gentle words.

"Let me guess." Will's mouth twitched as if he were holding back a laugh. "You figured out I run on the beach with Prince and decided to set up an accidental meeting in hopes of gleaning secret information from me as our friendship naturally developed."

My jaw dropped a bit, but I quickly recovered and faked a yawn. I scrambled for a comeback after he'd effectively taken a knife to my plans and ripped them open to reveal all my secrets, which were obviously terrible if he'd guessed them the first try. So there would be no stealth and mystery of an undercover operation. I'd have to be more upfront, like Will. He clearly loved the shock factor. I'd have to take a play from his book.

"Hardly. I already know all about you," I said, my voice shaky at first. "I know about your family. And I know we're mortal enemies and you're most likely plotting to kill me." The last few words came out in a whoosh. Hopefully, he'd take the bait.

Will withdrew his hand from my arm as he choked on his coffee.

Bingo. But hell. Why stop there? What better place to make decisions than with the Parthenon behind me? Big places were meant for big decisions. "I know you were in Paris and set up Jolie to find my mom. I know you shot at me and Malcolm and tried to kill me when I jumped on Jolie." My hand instinctively went to rub my leg where the bullet had been. I turned to him. "Why don't we be honest and stop the act. I know you're not this flirty fun loving care free guy and you probably can't stand the fact that your hair is in your face."

Will pressed his lips together and placed his coffee on the cracked pavement. His chest heaved and I thought for sure he was having heart failure at my stupidity. But instead he laughed again, like he did at the beach. A hearty laugh. After a couple minutes he wiped his eyes.

"You know what, Savvy Bent? Want to know the truth?" The moon revealed his chiseled features.

"What?"

"I like you."

"Okay." I drew the word out, not sure how to respond, not sure if he was counteracting my bluntness with a compliment.

"And I understand why my foolish brother fell head over heels for you."

I sucked in my breath at the mention of Malcolm. Head over heels?

Then his phone chirped from his pocket. He held up a finger. "I have to get this."

He opened his phone and stepped away a few paces. I wanted to claw my eyes out at my stupid impulses. But I couldn't stand any more lies and games. I wanted truth. I needed truth. And at that point, I'd do anything to get it.

Will returned a couple minutes later. He slipped his phone into his pocket. "We have to head back. You know, the family business calls." He winked and laughed again. "As I was saying, I like you. You're honest and brave. I have an offer for you."

"Thanks for the compliment." An offer? Adrenaline raced through my veins at what he might say.

"Let's get back to the car first." With a light hand on my back, he guided us forward.

We headed back down the hill, through the narrow streets of the market places and back to his car. After about ten minutes of driving he finally talked.

He rubbed his chin. "I have a deal for you, Savvy Bent. You can take it or leave. I'll give you twenty-four hours to decide and then it's off the table."

I stared, needles prickling along my shoulders at what he might say. "What is it?"

"I'll offer you complete safety, no more hiding out and living in fear. That includes your mom, and your dad. But you need to live with my parents, my grandmother and me. I'll train you. Teach you the secrets of self-defense."

I gripped the sides of the leather seat and stared at him in shock. No more hiding out or living in fear? Safety? I was definitely interested.

"I know. I rather surprised myself too. But, like I said, this is a one-time offer."

This was what I wanted. This was what I'd worked so hard for in Paris. But then the realization hit that he'd want something in return. "What's the catch?"

"Nothing comes without a price. I get the extreme satisfaction of keeping a close eye on my enemy, and we might need you to do some work for us on the side. Nothing major."

The twinkle in his eyes made me think he didn't mean sweeping the kitchen floor. I stared out the car window and imagined Malcolm sitting in his boat playing solitaire or sharpening his knives. Whatever assassins do in their spare time. What would he think?

"I won't kill anyone."

He smiled. "No problem."

I narrowed my eyes. "How do I know this isn't a trick to lure me into your house and slit my throat in my sleep?"

He burst out with a deep, belly laugh. "Sweet thing, if I wanted you dead, I wouldn't have to lure you into my house." He lost any humor and turned threatening. "Regardless of what you and your mother might think, we don't kill for fun or without purpose. We work and live above the emotion. The people that lose their lives from the blade of my knife deserve it."

I shivered and clamped my teeth together to keep them from rattling. I needed to tack on one more addendum. "I also want the complete protection of one Constance Gerald."

He blinked away the annoyance that flashed across his face. "Fine. You've got it. I'll need your answer by tomorrow night before sundown."

I spent the rest of the drive lost in my thoughts and the ludicrousness of his idea that I was contemplating.

We drove through familiar streets. "I have to cut the evening short. Duty calls. Do you want me to swing you by your house?"

"You can drop me off a little down the street." From there I'd head down to the shore. I couldn't go home. But I couldn't just go straight to his house either. I needed to think.

Not far from my house, he slowed the car to a stop. With a quick salute, he said, "I hope to see you by tomorrow night." He held out a phone. "Don't worry it's a cheap extra. Our residence here in Greece is programmed into the GPS system."

We said goodbye. After his taillights disappeared, I headed to the sea to air out my thoughts. The cool breeze and briny smell welcomed me. I waited a bit, then said, "You can come out now."

Adamos appeared from the darkness as usual. "We need to talk."

I flashed him a wry grin. No kidding.

Eleven

ADAMOS APPROACHED, HIS DARK clothing perfect for sneaking around in the night. His arms were stiff at his sides. No trace of a smile crossed his face, and his eyes had lost the normal glint of pride and protection he felt toward me.

I sighed and rubbed a chill from my arms. "You don't have to tell me what's at stake here. I know."

He stood next to me, with his arms crossed and stared out over the sea, his jaw firm, his forehead creased. "Tell me then."

"What?"

"Tell me exactly what's at stake." His soft voice weakened my defenses.

I refrained from calling my mom's new friend Birdman or the Blob and sighed. "Constance is a target and it's our duty to protect him and that's what my mom's been doing, putting her work first, putting his safety and protection first, following through with the supposed calling on our family. I get it. Okay?" I stood and headed toward home.

Adamos matched me stride for stride. "You never asked to be thrust into the middle of this fight. I understand." He left his thoughts dangling, filled with the unspoken conclusion that I'd made the wrong decision.

Adamos always made quiet suggestions, and left me to piece together the wisdom. But this time, I'd made up my mind. Nothing would change that but it was my turn to leave him with my cryptic thoughts.

"I have to do my part but that doesn't include hiding in my room because Mom wants to be the sacrificial parent. I'm not going to help by spending all my time watching birds and keeping company with a total slime ball."

Adamos nodded, soaking in the realization that I wasn't going to sit back anymore begging for crumbs of attention or information from Mom.

"I proved in Paris that I can make my own decisions and I can here too." My arms trembled with the adrenaline surge that came with risky choices, but I meant every word. I'd do this my way, even if all I wanted to do was run away with Malcolm. I'd go home and after Mom went to bed, I'd pack and slip out the window.

He was slow to answer on the trip back. We walked side-by-side, in silence, drifting through the streets as shops closed for the day and the nightlife kick started. Close to home, he finally stopped.

"I'm not in the position to warn you on the risks of what you're considering." His carefully guarded emotions peeled back to reveal the soft underside of my Greek bodyguard. Past regrets and mistakes lingered in his expression as he talked. "I left my faith, my brethren, for what I felt was a new calling that I couldn't ignore. My brothers laughed at my visions and scoffed at my emerging beliefs in what they meant. Eventually, I stopped sharing with them and formed plans." He paused and glanced toward the lights in my home, the silhouette of Mom in the window. "I will never play God with you. But think carefully before you live with your enemy. Make sure it is your only choice."

With that, he squeezed my hand and then faded into the shadows surrounding my house. Was this my only choice? No. I could run away with Malcolm, which when I allowed myself to fantasize about that, a thrill of anticipation ran through me. But I didn't want to run away. I could continue to hang out with Mom and wait for a chance to prove myself. But that could take years.

After another ten minutes of debating, I decided to talk with Mom one last time, beg her to include me and answer my questions. I strode up the tiny stone walkway and entered through the front door.

"Good evening, Savvy."

Mom sat on the couch, a suitcase at her feet. She smiled but it wasn't the kind of smile that said welcome home. More like she'd made a decision and knew I wouldn't like it. A cold anger strained her face: her eyelids twitched and her nostrils flared every few seconds. She clasped her hands tight in her lap, her fingers a dull white from the pressure. She'd obviously checked my room and figured out I'd rebelled and left without her permission.

Any thoughts of asking and begging faded. A fresh stubbornness emerged, stronger than ever, and I gained a new confidence behind my decision.

"Going away for an overnight with Constance?" I asked, playing a dangerous game.

"No, Savvy." She didn't try to hide the hurt in her eyes at my barb.

I clapped my hands with fake glee. "Are we visiting Dad?" When she shook her head no, I said, "I know we're not leaving Athens because you'd never leave a job unfinished. So please, tell me, I can't bear the suspense."

She spoke in her quiet but stern mom voice. "I've contacted a friend in England who owes me a favor. He's agreed to take you in until this ordeal is over and I can meet you there."

I opened my mouth to argue but she cut me off.

"You will be perfectly safe. I made a foolish mistake by bringing you here, thinking I could shelter you from everything. But," her voice softened, "I wanted to spend time with you, even if it hasn't been much." She cleared her throat as if emotion had nothing to do with this. "There will be no debate. Your plane leaves within the hour."

While I gathered my last few items and shoved them in a backpack, Mom didn't leave my side. I was surprised my window wasn't boarded up with plywood. The only alone time I managed was when Mom used the bathroom right before we left. I sprinted to the counter and rummaged through her purse. Sweat prickled my armpits with the heat of possibly getting caught as I scrolled through her recent emails. My eyes darted across the messages until I found the right one. Quickly, my fingers flew over the keypad. The toilet flushed and the water ran in the sink. I had seconds.

The door squeaked open on its hinges. I pressed send, deleted the correspondence, then powered down the phone and dropped it in her purse. When she walked into the room and picked up her purse and keys, I pretended to fumble with the straps of my backpack and flashed her a weak smile.

We said nothing in the cab ride to the airport. I could've thrown a fit, stomped my feet, screamed, refused to go, but I had a plan. Throngs of people crowded the lobby of the airport, their laughter and cries of goodbye only digging at my heart. When my flight number blared over the intercom, we briefly hugged. She ran down the list of shallow regrets and encouraged me to be on my best behavior. We decided it was best to communicate through email so as not to drum up an expensive phone bill. I agreed.

I turned to the gate, inching along, waiting for her to leave.

My heart beat loud and fast, daring me to follow through with my plans, to rebel in the worst way. A smirk tugged at my lips as I thought back to the email I'd sent to the kind Mr. Rottingham of England from my mom. In the message, Mom profusely apologized for the inconvenience, but her plans had changed and I would not be visiting him. She hoped at some point in the future they could all visit and drink tea together while watching a game of Polo.

I left the airport and hailed the first cab that drove by.

An hour later, I stood on the docks watching Malcolm's boat move with the waves. Moonlight reflected off the Mediterranean. Boats rocked. Sails gently flapped on the ocean breeze. I'd made a decision on the hillside near the mighty Parthenon and I was going with my plan, with my own special style, for better or worse.

Mom and Malcolm would never know until I succeeded in my mission and revealed everything. Then I'd be praised for my valiant efforts, my sins forgotten.

I strode down the dock, climbed on Malcolm's boat and ripped open the cabin door. He whipped out a gun and had it aimed at my heart within seconds.

"Damn it, Savvy." He put the weapon away. "Be careful who you sneak up on."

"Sorry!" I quickly found a seat across from him. "I wanted to stop in and say hello." The truth? I needed to say goodbye because I was going deep on the dangerous side of a mission that I couldn't tell him about.

He guzzled a bottle of water then leaned forward with light in his eyes. "Okay, so you've thought about my plan?"

"Yes, I've thought about it."

"Terrific. I have a great way to just disappear." He pulled me close, and his lips brushed against my skin. He snapped his fingers. "Just like that. No one will ever know."

For a brief second, my resolve wavered as he traced his fingers down my arm. I had to correct him before he tempted me even more. "I've thought about it, but not in the way you think. I can't run away."

He jerked away, and his face lost its optimism and light. He leaned back and crumpled the plastic bottle in his fist.

I started babbling, words tumbling out, as I laid my heart on the table. "Not that I wouldn't want to run away with you, away from all this mess and start over. It would be great. You and me. No worries. I could go back to before all this happened, before this nightmare started. Except I'd have you with me." I bit my lip. "I can't leave my mom."

"I guess I understand. I've been in this a lot longer than you have. I'm ready to leave it behind." He sighed. "It was just me wishing, dreaming of the way I wish life could be. We have a lot of catching up to do but I haven't stopped thinking about you since Paris. We need a chance, away from our families."

My breath caught. "I'm sorry," I whispered. "Maybe down the road, later on." Then I finished off what I came to say. This was the hard part because every word of it was a lie. "I think it's best if we don't see each other. Until this is all over, that is." More like he couldn't find out I was heading to his home, invading his territory, spying on his family. Hopefully, he'd stay mad at his family until I completed my mission.

He jerked his head up. "What?"

I closed my eyes, fighting against what my heart wanted, which was to forget all this nonsense with Will and take off with Malcolm. But I knew that dream wouldn't last. Life always catches up. "This is goodbye."

Twelve

WITH THE GPS SYSTEM on the phone offering its dim light, I headed away from the sea and the narrow streets and into a more residential area filled with beautiful homes. The big white colonial houses rose up around me like pale ghosts in a graveyard. If anyone peered out from behind their curtains, they'd see my phone light bobbing about like a firefly. An easy target. My enemies could see me coming a mile away. Maybe that was the plan. I shivered and glanced back into the darkness, praying Adamos was close behind.

Scattered amongst the fancy southern colonial-like houses were white washed homes with original architecture, well-placed shrubbery and landscaping. They weren't quite so tall but referred more to the flavor of Athens and the surrounding towns. Still gorgeous.

I glanced at the GPS. I'd arrived. Their home, my new home, fit in with the rest of them, nothing conspicuous that said assassins live here. An outside light shone down on potted plants, and ferns piled around the front door. In the small side yard, water spurted out the mouth of a Greek goddess and splashed into a pool of water.

I hesitated at the bottom step leading to the door. What would I say to Malcolm's parents? "Hey, you know me, I'm your enemy. Don't worry Will invited me; and no, I don't plan on spying on you at all. Don't worry about it."

Yeah, somehow I didn't see any line I could conjure up working well.

A ferocious barking was followed by Prince bounding around the side of the house, teeth bared, slobber flying. Instinctively, I moved my suitcase in front of me and bit back a scream. He bounded across the grass, covering the ground before I could even think to run. He stopped a few feet in front of me, lowered his body close to the ground and growled.

"Nice doggie. Good doggie. Remember me?" I inched back toward the fountain. "I threw you the tennis ball, you jogged through the sand, the sun on your, um, hair or fur whatever is you have. You liked me, I promise. We had an immediate connection."

He didn't seem to believe me or remember our bonding because his growl intensified and his eyes stayed focused on me. Why didn't I think to bring dog biscuits or something?

"Come on, Prince. I'm shocked and hurt you don't remember." I stepped up onto the edge of the fountain, pulling up my bag after me. "I'm really a cheery sort of gal when you get to know me." I flashed him a cheesy grin. "Come on, look at my smile. Doesn't it say, 'trust me'?"

"Is that how you deal with all your enemies?" Will stepped from the shadows.

Relief flooded me. "Um, can you call off the attack dog?"

Will rubbed his chin in a way that reminded me of Malcolm. His hair no longer flopped about his face but was slicked back and instead of the casual clothes of a California dude he looked more like an uptight banker, or an assassin. He snapped his fingers and Prince whined, but then jogged back to the house. With a wave of his hand, Will motioned me inside. I stepped down from the fountain, my legs shaking, and obeyed. He led me into the house and through the kitchen with gleaming granite countertops and stained wood cupboards, where I couldn't help but notice the lemon bars.

Will cleared his throat so I dragged myself away from the kitchen and padded down the short hallway. He sighed and looked rather bored, like I was just some kind of inconvenience.

I followed the direction of his pointing fingers into the room and dropped my suitcase. A witty joke I'd thought up on the way over lay on the tip of my tongue ready to ease the tension and bring a smile to his face—like remember not to kill me in the middle of the night—but when I turned around he was gone.

I quickly changed as exhaustion from the day stole over me, and pulled me toward the bed. I shut the door, then grabbed a simple wooden chair from the desk and propped it under the doorknob. I was pretty sure that trick actually worked. Then I curled up under the down comforter with all its softness and just-washed scent and I snuggled into it and tried to fall asleep. But living in a house with my mortal enemies had a way of playing with my mind. Every creak and nighttime rattle was Will ready to infiltrate my room, knife at the ready. Not sure how long I stared at the doorknob, waiting for it to move.

Before I knew it, Prince was scratching at my door, growling. I mumbled and then rolled over, hiding under the sheets.

Someone banged on the door. "Up and at 'em. First day of training. Time for a run."

I groaned.

"You've got two minutes to be outside ready to go."

The clock read 4:30. Holy cow. Dad would be in absolute heaven that I was waking up and running at this god-awful time of the morning. I stumbled about for the light switch, which then blinded me for a few minutes as I zipped open my suitcase and pulled out running shorts and a T-shirt. I shuffled outside and hoped my clothes weren't inside out or backward.

I breathed in the cool morning air laced with the scent of hyacinth flowers and told myself I could handle this. In the driveway, Will stood shoulder to shoulder with Malcolm, chatting, well, like brothers. If I'd been half asleep before, I was wide awake now, my nervous energy and guilt skyrocketing.

Malcolm wasn't supposed to know anything about my plans. I'd said my goodbyes last night. He'd think everything was a lie.

They didn't even glance back. Will wore a casual business suit and Malcolm's workout clothes made my heart pulse faster. I completed several deep knee lunges in the effort to look cool and get my body to a functioning capacity, while my brain tried to process this change of events. Will finally spoke, his words sharp and to the point.

"I have business to take care of early this morning. Malcolm," he couldn't keep the snideness from tainting his tone, "will be training you today. I'll be back for breakfast."

Malcolm winked and said, "Try and keep up."

"Hi to you too!" I called out, my words dripping sarcasm, angry that Malcolm had somehow known about my plan.

He took off running. I mean like really running, not even a warm up jog, but I didn't dare complain. I tried to pace myself but it was dark and I didn't want to lose him so I raced through the streets.

I pictured Mom about to wake up for her morning coffee, blocked any guilt and put the effort into running. The reasons for my screwed-up family ran through my mind. It all came back to Malcolm's family. The familiar bitter dislike toward them rose in my chest like a panic attack. Somehow I'd have to plaster on a smile and fake it. Then when I'd found evidence, I could return home and Mom would forgive everything. With every slap of my sneaker against the pavement, I convinced myself that was how it would all play out.

We left his neighborhood and eventually entered the narrow streets closer to the sea. Shops were still closed and only our feet echoed instead of the slamming open of doors and the chatting of customers.

Miles passed under my feet, or it felt like miles. I didn't mind it at first. The crisp air was quite invigorating and my blood started pumping. But he didn't stop. He kept going and going, arms swinging like a maniac. Invigorating soon turned into sharp cramps and gasping for breath. Malcolm didn't look back once. With sweat soaking through my tee and dripping down my back, I pushed harder. He couldn't just leave me behind.

But he did. Two seconds later, his bobbing head disappeared.

I slowed and stopped, hunching over, sucking in air like a wheezing grandma. The streets seemed emptier, the air chilly as my sweat dried. Sounds I didn't notice when running became sharp and distinct. A shutter from a shop window slamming open in the breeze. A motorcycle buzzing in the distance. Footsteps.

Wait. Footsteps?

I got a second wind and took off after Malcolm. My heart beat fast but not because of my sudden sprint. I ducked down a side street, trying to shake off the creep factor. When I reached the top of a hill, overlooking the Mediterranean, I slowed. My legs were cooked spaghetti and I was ready to collapse. I sank onto the ground and didn't hold back the sob.

Shoes crunched the gravel near me. I snapped to attention and peered through blurry vision.

"Malcolm?" I croaked, relief sweeping through me.

"Yeah, it's me." He sat next to me, arms folded across his chest, a grim look on his face.

Silence wedged between us and I didn't know where to start. How would I explain my deception and betrayal?

He spoke in this sweet, high lilting voice, mocking me. "I just can't leave yet, Malcolm. I can't leave my family. I don't think we can see each other until this is over."

I bit my lip, holding back a laugh, because I knew he was serious.

"What were you thinking? Moving in with my family?" he asked, his eyes searching mine for the truth. "Are you crazy?"

"I'm sorry. I wanted to tell you, but I figured you'd put a stop to it somehow."

"Damn right, I would've. You don't know my brother." He turned so he was directly facing me. "You should've just told me the truth."

I half-smiled, trying to lighten the mood. "How'd you find out?"

"Oh, that one's easy. Will called me to gloat to say my little girlfriend just made a deal with them and was moving in."

The air left my chest in one big whoosh. "Jeez. He didn't wait very long. So much for my plans."

Malcolm reached over and took my hand in his. My heart fluttered. "That's why I came back. For you. I couldn't leave you unprotected in this pack of wolves."

I wanted to reach over and hug him but I'd effectively told him that our relationship needed to wait. "Thanks."

He stood and stretched both his arms. "But that doesn't mean I'll take it easy on you. You asked for this, you wanted this, you'll get it." He nudged my leg with the toe of his sneaker. "Time to go." Then he took off.

Thirteen

MALCOLM SHOWED NO MERCY during the sprint back. I limped into the house about ten minutes late and then spent too long in the hot shower, the water pelting my sore back and aching leg muscles. After a longing look at my rumpled bed, I headed to the kitchen, hoping Malcolm would be there for introductions.

The smell of coffee brewing made me weak in the knees. I caught a whiff of cinnamon and fantasized about sweet rolls or some Greek dish I'd never heard of, but the closer I got to the kitchen, the slower I walked.

Did his whole family eat breakfast together? What if Will's father took the opportunity to throw a kitchen knife through my chest? Knowing Will, they would do it all in the name of training. As they leaned over my body, blood seeping from my chest, they'd say, "It was training, Savvy. We wanted to work on your reflexes but you moved too slowly. Sorry."

For the first time, I wished I'd had time to grab my cache of spy gadgets before Mom whisked me away to Greece. The fern in the hallway would be perfect to place a bug. Or a picture frame with a hidden video cam on the kitchen counter might ease my nerves.

With that thought I stopped at the edge of the hallway, listening. Their voices and laughter melted together, sounding surprisingly happy for assassins.

"Who's there?" a sharp peppery voice asked.

My mouth went dry and my knees shook. With a sigh and a glance up to heaven at my spy ancestors, I strode into the kitchen with a slight swagger to show the confidence I lacked.

"Finally!" An elderly woman with white hair rapped her knuckles against the table. "You strain your back? You're walking funny."

I stopped the swagger. Will or Malcolm weren't anywhere to be seen. Their mother stood behind the bar flipping fresh French toast onto a plate. Her shoulder-length black hair was streaked with sliver. The red scoop neck shirt told me she dressed nice but wasn't hoity toity. She smiled and winked at me.

"Welcome, Savvy. I'm Janelle."

I nodded, relieved to see a smile. "Hi."

The elderly woman spoke again. "We've been waiting."

I wondered if I could knock her over with one breath. She might look frail but I sensed she was a tower of strength. I'd want her on my side.

Someone mumbled from behind the newspaper and flicked the top right corner as if waving.

"Bartholomew," Janelle said sternly.

He grumbled again.

Janelle strode over and ruffled his hair. "We have company." She patted his shoulders. "This is Will and Malcolm's father."

"What, oh, um, right." He folded down the newspaper and studied me with his dark eyes, his eyebrows lowered. He looked like an older version of Malcolm with lines on his forehead and around his eyes and the start of a paunchy belly.

"And be nice." Janelle went back to the French toast. She pointed at the grandmother. "And that goes for you too, Edith."

A rumbling noise came from Bartholomew's throat and he put away the newspaper. "You don't look much like a mortal enemy."

The grandmother rapped her knuckles again. "Don't let her fool you. She foiled your plans in Paris." She narrowed her eyes. "Looks can be deceiving. We'll have to keep our eyes on this one."

I stood paralyzed by the table, taking them all in, shocked at how normal it all felt. French toast. The dad reading the newspaper, just like mine. The crotchety grandmother. What had I expected? For them to juggle knives over a bowl of Frosted Flakes?

"Don't you talk, girl?" Bartholomew asked.

"Be nice. This is only her first day." Janelle reminded them.

The grandmother pointed to a chair next to her. "Might as well sit down. Next to me. Easier to see you." She jabbed her crooked finger at me. "Troublemaker I tell you."

I stumbled over to the long wooden table. Overwhelmed. That would describe what I was feeling perfectly.

"Um, good morning," I said with probably a bit too much cheer. What do I say to the family who tried to kill me last year? And might try again at some point in the future.

Bartholomew lifted his arms. "She talks. Finally."

They all started eating, and I stared at the blank space in front of me. Should I serve myself? Or wait? My stomach growled.

"Sorry, dear." Janelle laid her napkin in her lap. "Will gave specific orders that you were under training and he was in charge of your diet. You'll have to wait for him."

My insides crumbled and I blinked against the burn in my eyes as I stared at the pile of toast oozing with gooey cinnamon sugar. Maple syrup practically flowed from a pewter server. Will bustled into the kitchen. He'd changed into black warm-ups and a wicking shirt. I wasn't sure what that meant for our after breakfast activities.

"Good morning!" he said with way too much enthusiasm.

"Good morning, dear. I think your guest is famished."

"Oh she's made of strong stuff," he said with his head in the fridge. "A little hunger won't kill her."

Edith snorted. Bartholomew burst out with a loud guffaw and Janelle giggled like a schoolgirl.

Edith spoke through her laughter, tiny chunks of chewed-up French toast splattering the table. "But we don't want to starve her to death."

The whole family burst out, their laughter rippling round the table and filling the kitchen. Bartholomew tried every few seconds to pull himself together but every time he opened his mouth to eat, he started laughing again.

I gripped the chair under the table and smiled through clenched teeth while my cheeks burned. They were joking. About my death.

"Oh, stop." Janelle struggled to compose herself but her shoulders shook. "This is just wrong. You'll give this poor girl the wrong impression."

"I think it's a little late for that." Will ran the blender after dumping in yogurt, strawberries and carrots. Then he carried over a glass full of his frothy concoction, a banana, and granola.

I brought it to my lips, then studied the drink a bit closer.

"Oh, please," Will said. "Poison isn't my style. You're safe to eat." He held up his hands, palms out. "Part of our deal."

I gulped down the health drink and peeled my banana. Seeing this family laugh like a pack of hyenas made me think of Malcolm's sly smile and his jokes. I totally got him. And it made me think of my family. The last time we ate a meal together and laughed was years ago. My appetite faded.

Bartholomew noticed and his laughter dwindled as if he sensed my mood. He coughed and straightened his back. "Sorry about that episode of bad behavior. Hazard of the business." He dabbed the corners of his mouth with his napkin. "So did Will put you through his famous early morning run?"

I nodded. "You could call it that."

I studied the family around me. These people, laughing and joking together, were assassins? They plotted and planned for months on the best way to kill someone in cold blood?

The bitterness rose again like bile in my throat. They'd shot at me in Paris so I knew they weren't all giggles and sunshine, but I just couldn't see it. Not this fun, happy family. Unless it was just part of some act to intimidate me.

Janelle cast a stern motherly look in Will's direction as he stacked ten pieces of French toast on his plate. "You know I don't approve of your games. Too early in the morning, and for Malcolm to leave her behind?" She shook her head in disapproval.

"That's right," Edith said.

"Well, you know I'm always open to suggestions. But so far, none of you have come up with anything better." Will popped an overloaded bite into his mouth.

"Bah!" Edith whipped the syrup away from him. "I say you should've brought her out to the middle of the Mediterranean and then," she lowered her voice, "when she least expected it, dumped her overboard. You could've held her under for a minute or so. That would put the fear of God in her."

I choked on my granola.

"Also could've killed her," he said dryly, "but maybe that wouldn't have been so bad."

Bartholomew started cackling again but after one look at me, toned it down. "Sorry about that."

We heard the whistle first and objects crashed through the windows of the house. Black containers rolled across the floor, immediately letting out smoke. The filmy wisps rose, threading between us, blinding our vision.

"Take cover!" roared Bartholomew. "And try not to breathe!"

Fourteen

THE WHOLE FAMILY MOVED into action. Edith scrambled for her cane. The dad pulled a pistol from a drawer in the table. Janelle grabbed the meat cleaver. Will shot from his chair and whipped his head back and forth, searching the exits, his face a mask of scary determination.

A masked man punched out the rest of the sliding glass door and crashed into the kitchen. I couldn't miss the knife clutched in his hand. Flashbacks of the catacombs in Paris and Adamos created a jelly-like sensation in my knees. The blood, the wet, slippery feel. The metallic smell hitting the back of my throat. The clenching of my stomach. The heartbreak. It all came back and I slithered to the floor and cowered under the table. I hugged my knees and closed my eyes.

But I couldn't block out the noise. The grunts. The groans. The crashing of objects being thrown. The landing of chairs. Something thumped next to me. Edith lay on her side, her eyes closed. Was she…? I shot my hand out to feel for a pulse in her neck, my fingers resting on her leathery skin. Still beating.

"Help them," she croaked. "They need you."

She pushed her cane toward me and I noticed the blade sticking out the end of it. I swallowed my breakfast back down, not able to reach out and grab the cane-turned-weapon. Smoke dried out the back of my throat and I coughed.

Slowly, I inched to the side and peered out. Janelle swung the broad-bladed knife back and forth, missing the guy but backing him toward her husband on the far left of the kitchen. He held a kitchen chair over his head. His gun gleamed from under the couch across the floor. Oh my spy gods. I tried to get Will's attention so he could find it but he lay slumped against the far wall off to the right. Blood dripped from the side of his head.

No. This couldn't be happening. As much as I hated this family, I loved Malcolm. And these people were his family. Through the ribbons of smoke, I could barely see Will, his face ashen, his body motionless. I crawled out from under the table and toward the gun. My hand itched just thinking about it. Tiny prickles of heat swarmed my skin from the top of my head to the tip of my toes.

Halfway between the kitchen table and the gun, I heard a thump and a crash. Janelle lay crumpled on the floor, deathly still. Fear wrapped around my neck, like hands squeezing, making it hard to breath. I froze, my eyes glued to Bartholomew, the last man standing. He brought the chair down on the guy who easily batted it away.

A shot echoed and Bartholomew grabbed his side and slammed against the wall. He slowly slid to the floor, his face contorted with pain.

Tears blurred my vision and I scrambled for the gun. My fingers were inches away when my stomach exploded in pain. The attacker kicked me again and I rolled. Gasping for breath, I struggled to my feet. He seemed to be toying with me, waiting to see what I would do. His foot shot out, and he kicked the gun to the other side of the room near Will.

Time stopped and I took inventory. Everyone was knocked out or dead. No one was left. Edith's whispered words echoed inside me while Will's ashen face reminded me of Malcolm's. The smoke was dissipating but I still couldn't see past my enemy's mask.

The man picked up a chair and launched it at me. I ducked but a leg caught the side of my head and knocked me off balance. I swear I heard him laugh which royally pissed me off.

"Coward!" I cried out.

Adrenaline surged through my arms and legs and I dropped to the ground. My fingers reached for Edith's cane.

All of sudden I was rushing at him. The room blurred, but this man remained perfectly clear, a dark target. A yell sounded off the walls and I realized it was me. In two steps I was at him, jabbing the cane. It plunged into his side.

He grabbed his gut and lifted it away with blood on his hand. "Hey!"

"Yeah, that's right, coward."

Then he took off back through the door and disappeared into the neighborhood. I stood, trembling amongst the rubble. Smoke lingered, carrying with it the sting of the attack and my cowardice. The bodies didn't move. A lamp lay in pieces. The truth of the situation and what happened weighed on me. Minutes ago I was eating breakfast with a friendly family of assassins and now they were all dead. My legs buckled and I fell to my knees.

"I'm sorry," I whispered. Silence filled the room. It felt like a tomb. Why did he spare me? Why did he run?

"No worries, dear." Janelle lifted her head and pushed off the floor. Her hair lay in tangles around her face. She smiled weakly.

Edith groaned. "Someone can at least help an old woman to her feet. I'm not quite as spry as I used to be."

Janelle moved to her side.

"I'm so sorry," I whispered again, glancing at Bartholomew. Tears rushed, no holding them back.

He grunted and waved his hand. "I'm alive!"

Relief whooshed through me.

"Will." Janelle spoke sternly and helped Edith to her feet. They both turned on him. "This is coming directly out of your bank account. All this damage. I want it cleaned up and everything replaced by dinner tonight."

What? How could they talk to their son like that when he was half alive?

Will wiped the blood from his face and smirked. "It was rather theatrical, wasn't it?"

Janelle's stern look broke up and she giggled. "Your best yet."

Thoughts entered my head. Theatrical? His best yet? "Are you people crazy? Your home is in ruins and you were just attacked."

"Will." Bartholomew spoke sternly as if his son were a toddler scribbling on the wall with a crayon.

"Fine, fine." He approached me. "This was officially your second training session. Planned by me for your benefit." He bowed.

Understanding dawned. My fingers trembled and one by one they curled into a fist. The whole thing, the smoke bombs, the attack, it was a set up. For me. For my training.

"Now I just need some hash browns to go with this fake blood." He licked his fingers.

The entire family cracked up. They relived the scene moment-by-moment, applauding Will for his work. Anger pulsed and it built in my fists. I stepped over the lamp and kicked Edith's cane aside. The family took one look at me, and their laughter died.

"Hey, Will."

He turned with a cocky grin, full of himself and congratulatory for pulling one over on me. My fist met his face. The impact sent pain rocketing back through my arm.

Fifteen

I STOMPED OUT THROUGH the jagged door and ran to the garden. The smell of the hyacinth mixed with the various smells of blooming flowers clashed with the rage welling within me. I stomped through flowerbeds and whirled around, wanting to shred all the tiny purple and yellow flowers. I breathed deep, trying to grasp everything that just happened.

Water trickling into the fountain pool broke through the haze of thoughts rapidly shooting through my brain. I moved toward the fountain, then dipped my throbbing knuckles into the pool, running them back and forth across the surface. First it was just my fingers drinking in the cool water but I sunk my hand lower and lower, the water a distraction from the horrific memory and my brain trying to wrap around the fact that it wasn't real. Not the blood. Not the gunshot. Not the attack.

I dropped to my knees, the gravel digging into my skin. I cupped my hands into the water and splashed my face. Once, then again. I scrubbed, erasing the memory of Edith falling to the floor next to me, croaking out for help; Janelle falling, and then the gunshot. And Will, his face, ash gray, and the blood coloring his skin like a three year old drew a long angry red line down his cheek. And it was all an act. I scrubbed harder. Splashed more.

And then a light touch was on my back.

"Don't touch me." The words shot from my mouth. I scrubbed harder because if I didn't release my aggression I wasn't sure what I would do.

Malcolm pushed me back from the fountain's edge. My shoulder grazed the rounded stones as I fell on my butt onto the gravel path. The small sharp stones dug into my hands. My hair wrapped in snake-like strands around my neck and shoulders. Water dripped between my shoulder blades.

"Stand up." His face was like a mask, cold and hard, no flicker of any emotion.

"No." I brushed off the excess water from my arms with jerky motions, refusing the angry tears trembling, ready to fall.

"Stand up and fight."

I glared, my eyes like slits, wanting to pummel him to the ground and into dust. He kicked me with his toe.

"You knew about this?" The words hissed through my clenched teeth.

"Get up and fight. Damn it!" he yelled and nudged me again, a little harder. "What? You thought training would be lifting weights and sparring with wooden poles? Maybe a leisurely trip to the target range? Sorry, sweetie. That's for the movies."

"You could've warned me about this," I spit out.

He laughed, the sound shallow. "Will has about a thousand ways of approaching training. I had no idea he'd pull this trick." His voice turned bitter. "He doesn't exactly confide in me."

The itch started in my fingers and spread up my arms. A feeling. A desire to hit, to scream, to run. The urge raced through my nerves, spreading, exploding. As soon as I got to my feet I lunged at him. My arms wrapped around his waist and we fell to the ground with a thud, his body a hard line underneath me.

"Is that all you got?" he gasped and pushed me off.

Back on our feet, I attacked again. Fists flying, I pounded his chest, his arms, his stomach. The fear, the shock, the anger released with every hit. He finally pushed me away and gave it back. He punched. I ducked. He kicked. I swerved to the side and took out the one leg he was standing on. We went at it. Both fighting. Sweat stung my eyes. Muscles burned and my lungs complained for air.

On my last lunge I clung, my arms wrapped around his chest, my body hanging off him.

"Keep going. If you're fighting for your life, no one's going to give you time to recover because you're past the point of exhaustion."

I swung but missed. He punched my arm.

"Use what you can. Find a weapon. Fists aren't all you have available and you won't always have your choice of knives or guns."

He punched again. My body cried out for relief. The tender spots throbbed where his fists had made contact. I wanted him to stop, for the garden to stop spinning. I stumbled away. Find a weapon. Find a weapon. Find a weapon. I crashed through the careful landscaping, tripping over the bushes. And then I saw it. A rake lay on the ground with nice pointed tines. I grabbed it and turned, my fingers digging into the wood.

Malcolm nodded in approval.

I rushed, jabbing the rake. He grabbed the end, right below the tines, and yanked me close. I stumbled. The rake fell and we landed in a heap in the grass. For the second time, I lay on top of him, breathing hard, wincing in anticipation of his harsh words or taunts. None came. His chest rose and fell. His breath hitched and the mask slipped and feeling flickered in his eyes. He didn't hate me and his lips were so close. Memories of our last kiss lingered and pulled me toward him.

But I rolled off, my chest heaving. The sky spun above, taunting me with her carefree attitude and light, wispy clouds. Every one of my bones cried out and my muscles complained. I couldn't move.

The clapping started softly at first and then grew. And then the whistles. I turned my head. Bartholomew, Janelle, Will and Edith stood at the edge of the yard, whistling and cheering. They meant to encourage and congratulate, but instead, each clap and whistle grated against my nerves, drawing up the bitterness from the deep well inside me.

"Savvy." Malcolm touched my arm, but I still couldn't find the strength to move.

His one word said more than any amount of words he could've strung together. Because words wouldn't be enough. Forced explanation wouldn't be enough. But in his voice I heard it. That he understood. That he'd been there. That this was his life, the death, the blood. I understood why he left his family and why he didn't want to betray them. I didn't want to know the kind of practical jokes they'd played on him in the name of training. All the stuff he could never explain to me. I got it.

"You're right," I said. "I saw training as jogging a couple miles. Learning to aim a gun. I didn't see the emotion behind it."

"That's just the first stage. You have to get to the point where you live and move and breathe beyond the emotion. On instinct. We have a very short time to train you. If Will had a year, you'd have some of those glorified training moments but from the little I've been told, there isn't a lot of time."

"What do you mean?" I pushed up to a sitting position. "Why?"

"Hey, I'm just the trainer. My family doesn't tell me everything either."

I flopped back down and stared back at the clouds dancing across the sky and hoped I hadn't made the biggest mistake of my life.

Sixteen

I'D HOPED THAT AFTER the first traumatic training session with the smoke bomb and fake blood that I'd get a break. I was wrong. It didn't matter where I was or my current activity status. In the shower. Eating lunch. Following my daily routine of sit-ups and push-ups. Flossing.

The lights would flick off and someone would attack, usually Malcolm, or he'd send me off on a trail of clues to rescue Edith. After a week or so I never knew when my head hit the pillow if I'd get a full night's sleep or not. Up was down and down was up. I ate muffins for dinner and spaghetti for breakfast. Or that was what it felt like. But if my family stayed safe and if I got a chance to peek at their deadly plans for Constance, it was worth it.

After one extremely exhausting early morning run, Malcolm pulled me aside after breakfast and said we had plans for the day. I didn't argue. Anything to escape the house for a little bit.

Within the hour, we were back at the dock. The mid-day sun glistened off the sides of the boats and sails winked out on the waters as if in on some cosmic joke. Malcolm rested his foot on the edge of his boat, his eyes piercing mine. My breath disappeared and my chest tightened. With his jeans and fit T-shirt I couldn't help but remember his melt-me-into-butter kisses.

"So, um, what's the plan? I know we're not here for a friendly outing," I said. He'd given no hint to our plans. Edith's ideas of training niggled in the back of my head. "You're not going to toss me overboard, are you?"

"We're on a recon mission. Jump aboard if you're coming."

I stepped on board with much reserve, wishing I'd worn my bathing suit under my clothes. He untied the boat and started the engine.

"Recon on what?" I called out over the motor.

"You'll see." Then with a mischievous smile, he guided the boat away from the dock.

I crossed my arms and puckered my lips into a pout. But it didn't last as the boat chugged out past the shallow waters, and he unfurled the sail. It snapped clean in the wind and we flew across the Mediterranean, the waves at our feet and the clouds our crown. I gripped the bench, completely enthralled.

I was flying, the air on my face, the wind in my hair, lifting off the anxiety of living and training with assassins.

Thirty minutes later, Malcolm slowed the boat, lowered the sails, and dropped anchor. The boat swayed with the swell of the waves, and the exhilaration I'd felt for the past half hour faded. I leaned against the hull so the sun could warm my face. The salt water brought back memories of family trips to the seashore, and I relaxed for the first time in a long time. Malcolm disappeared inside the cabin and returned holding a camera with a super zoom lens.

He pointed across the water toward the closest island. "I'm taking pictures of the monastery."

"Oh." So maybe my mission had to do with the monks instead of Constance? The same monks who wanted to kill us? My voice shook. "What are we going to do? Invade?"

"Need to know basis." He aimed the camera and started clicking.

"Does Will know I'm out here with you? Maybe he had some intense muscle training planned for me."

Malcolm didn't lower the camera. "Will went out of town. I'm in charge."

I repressed a shudder at what "business" took Will out of town. I focused on Malcolm instead. The wind tossed his hair about his face and pressed his T-shirt against his chest. I inched across the bench, a bit closer to where he stood, close enough to reach out and trace my fingers down his arm.

"Um, Malcolm?"

"Yeah?"

"Tell me about your childhood. Did you ever play Little League? Or go to Cub Scouts?"

"If I tell you, I might have to kill you." He smirked and I stuck my tongue out at him. He zoomed the lens out even more and kept clicking.

"Seriously. Was it hard?"

Finally, he lowered the camera and stared at the white caps, a distant look in his eyes, like he was in a different place and time. "We traveled a lot. Of course, I didn't know why until I was much older." He put the camera away and zipped the bag, then pulled out a picnic basket stored under one of the seats.

"Any strawberry tarts in there?" I asked, teasing, referring to our first date in Paris. We'd experienced only moments of a normal date before his brother ruined it with open fire in an effort to warn Malcolm to stay away from me.

"Not quite," he said, his voice on the edge of breaking into a laugh.

We sat on a blanket, our backs against the padded bench, and shared Malcolm's snack of grapes, bread, cheese and crackers. He cracked open two beers and handed me one. I sipped, the cold beer coating my parched throat. I pressed for more answers.

"What's your favorite memory, outside of training to throw knives and shoot a gun?"

"Lots of games," he said. "My dad would create games of logic for Will and I to play against each other. He wanted us to feel that competitive edge and be able to reason out all the sides of an issue before making a move."

"Hmm. Training in the form of games. Sounds fun." I waited and then said, "Not."

He laughed, his dimples flashing. "Okay, Miss Only Child. Let me guess. You spent your time playing Scrabble or going for family walks in the park." He waited and then said, "Boring."

I punched him. "Hey. Scrabble's fun." I laughed, but it trailed off, leaving me hollow on the inside. I thought about the last time we'd played a game as a family. Or taken a walk. It had been years.

He squeezed my hand. "Sorry. Maybe we should talk about something else."

But our easy conversation dwindled. His thumb traced over my hand, and my pulse jumped. I missed this. Just being together. Talking. Laughing. Being friends. The week or so of training hadn't left much time. "Do you ever think what your life would be like if your family weren't in their line of work?"

"Sure."

"Do you think we'd be together?" I swallowed my nerves. "Would you want to be with me?" The words choked in my throat. I not only missed our friendship, I missed him. Everything about him. His smile. His charcoal-flecked eyes. His touch. The way his face lit up when he looked at me. My heart missed him.

He didn't answer my question. His eyes captured mine, the charcoal flecks darkening. Instinctively, I reached up and traced my fingers across his lips, wishing I could lean in all the way to press mine to his.

"What do you want, Savvy?" he asked, guarded.

I let my hand drop and swayed forward. "I was lying to myself when I thought I could do this without you, I mean, without us, being together." I spoke softly. "I've missed you."

He closed the gap, our faces, our lips, inches apart.

"Sometimes I just want to forget," I said, my heart at a constant flutter.

"I can help you with that."

And then we were kissing. He pulled me closer, one hand entwined in my hair while the other pulled down the strap of my sundress. The breeze tickled my back while Malcolm's lips played with the skin on my neck. We forgot about time, lost in each other, both leaving behind our struggles. The boat rocked when a group of jet skis passed, but we didn't look. Another sailboat must've passed and men whistled and cheered. We ignored them.

But somewhere between the whispered apologies and kisses, Malcolm's back stiffened and he pulled away.

"What?" I had him back for a moment but the mask slid over his face again and I could feel him slipping away.

His hands skimmed my arms and his voice lowered. "I don't know if I could ever be everything you need me to be." He looked at me, his jaw firm. "And I don't want to put you in danger by association of my family and what we are, or have you caught in the middle."

I held my breath, not wanting to hear his next words.

He cupped my face with his hands and kissed me one last time. "My family will always find a way to drag me back into their lives. This time, it was through you."

"Oh." I hadn't thought about that. Will had used my relationship with Malcolm to bring him home and back to the family business, and it had worked.

He closed up the basket and stored it under the seat. He unfurled the sails, and I wrapped the blanket around me as we headed back to shore. Inside, my hopes and dreams deflated at his words. I couldn't speak or my voice would crack and the tears I furiously blinked away would fall. He didn't think our relationship could weather our family's hatred for each other. He was probably right.

Seventeen

TWO DAYS LATER, I sat in my chair, like a steel rod had been shoved along my spine. If I slouched the tiniest bit, the cane rapped on the floor and that cane scared the hell out of me. At Janelle's instructions, I tilted my head just so and plastered on a smile. My emotions were tucked away in a secret place that I could visit when I wanted, but for the most part I stayed away from that place because I couldn't bear to think about what could've been.

Edith sat in an overstuffed chair in the corner of the room, her cane at the ready, while Janelle sat directly across from me at a tiny glass table in a sunroom. Light poured through the skylights and windows, creating a happy glow. Potted ferns and exotic plants crowded the walls and corners of the room. A serving tray lay on a table laden with cucumber sandwiches, fruit salad and tiny cookies. And I'd thought I'd seen all the rooms in the house.

Janelle spoke in soft tones, elegance draped on her like a fancy woman's scarf bought from Paris. Instead of telling me to act, she was showing me and expecting me to respond. I felt kinda silly.

"Have you enjoyed the weather recently?" she asked, her teacup poised between her fingers.

"Um." All I could think about were my midnight sprints in the rain the past few nights.

The cane rapped on the floor.

I sat even straighter if that was possible. "Why yes, it has been rather wet."

"What kind of nonsense is that?" Edith called out. "Wet?"

"Well, except when I'm inside and then it's quite dry." I pinched a sandwich between my fingers and a cucumber plopped to the floor.

Janelle rubbed her temples. Edith mumbled and grumbled about dumping me in the Mediterranean, which seemed to be her constant threat.

"Okay, dear," Janelle said. "Never mind about the sandwich. Pretend you're sitting with a friend, chatting casually about school. Don't think of this as a performance." She tapped her chin. "Think of this as survival."

Huh?

"You slip at these luncheons or dinner parties," a fake smile crept onto her face and her eyes turned cold and heartless, "and it could mean your life and in your case that could also mean the life of your mother and father because without you they have no protection from us."

My hand trembled and the tea sloshed around in my cup. The emotions from my hidden place leaked out and reminded me of all I'd lost and the anger I felt against this family who controlled my life. Even though I'd accepted Will's deal, he'd played me like a lovesick fool.

"Oh, yes." Janelle sipped from her iced tea. "Emotion will happen. Messy heartbreaking emotion that makes you want to crumble and cry right there on the spot. Because if your enemy has done research, he'll know who you are, he'll know your weak spots, your Achilles' heel. He'll use that and purposefully jab into those soft spots with his words. Because if you're unnerved, he can best you. You'll screw up. And that's what he wants."

The cane rapped. "Start again."

Janelle crossed her legs and folded her hands in her lap. "What brought you to Athens? I see you're not a native."

"Well, you see," I paused, desperately seeking for the right words. "I'm here on summer vacation."

The cane rapped and Edith snorted. "It's spring."

I hunched over. "I can't do this."

Janelle reached across the table and held my hand, not grimacing at my sweaty palms. "Yes, you can do this. You must." She pulled her hand away. "So what brings you to Athens?"

I hesitated, crippled with fear at the stupid words I might utter. For a brief second, I closed my eyes and breathed deep, searching for something to say. "I'm visiting my uncle."

Janelle's eyes lighted with approval. "What does your uncle do? Maybe I've heard of him."

I laughed even though it sounded a bit forced. "I've been trying to figure that out myself. He keeps his business private." And this was the truth. I was visiting them for a brief stay and I couldn't break through to their secrets for the life of me. Maybe that was what I needed to do. Take my truths and twist it for the situation with vague answers that don't reveal a thing. Easier said than done.

"What about holding silverware and that kind of stuff?" I asked, twisting my napkin in my lap.

Janelle waved her hand. "No time. Small etiquette mistakes will slip by unnoticed but a show of nerves by bumbling your speech will be the death of you."

Bartholomew barged into the room. "Did I hear something about death?" Then he noticed me. "Are you two giving her a hard time? You know what Will said."

Janelle smiled, stood, and gracefully approached her husband. "Of course, we're giving her a hard time, dear. That's what we do, right?"

He winked at me. "Let me know if you need any info. Edith is a sucker for love, and my wife here loves a challenge. That would be you." He pointed to Edith. "Are you behaving yourself, Mother?"

"Of course."

Edith had it down pat. The confident answers. The lies. The image. She emphasized and took advantage of her ornery nature and her age. Janelle was a middle-aged mom who could sweet talk a cactus into giving up its needles. Both of them, inside, were tough. They had to be. I had to be.

"I'll be in my office. I'll catch you at dinner." He kissed Janelle and squeezed her butt. Not what I wanted to see.

She swatted his hand away, then patted her hair. "Are we set for our dinner plans this weekend?"

Bartholomew nodded. "Everything is set."

They closed the conversation. I didn't feel rejected that I wasn't invited. I saw opportunity. To sneak inside the office and look again for clues, something that betrayed their plans.

Eighteen

A FEW DAYS PASSED as I waited for the weekend and the opportunity to snoop, but it felt like forever. I followed the same meticulous routine over and over of running in the morning and at night. Only one other midnight run but I was beginning to adjust to those. I'd get up, run, then fall back into bed and sleep. I maintained a strict diet of only healthy food, except when I sneaked down to the kitchen in the middle of the night for cookies and lemon bars.

I took out my frustration and poured it into training. It was all business. I started every morning exhausted and I ended each day exhausted. And just like them, I learned to keep my private thoughts and emotions, my heartache, my fear and anger, tucked away inside where only I could access them. No longer were they written on my face like a child's messy sidewalk chalk drawing.

After just the past couple weeks, I was stronger. When I made a muscle in the mirror, a little bump formed. My whole body was more toned and ready. For what? I wasn't sure.

They weren't telling me anything. And something was brewing. I could tell by the stormy looks that crossed Bartholomew's face at odd moments of the day when he thought no one was looking. Edith attacked her knitting like a dog with a raw bone, making some god-awful puke green sweater. And Janelle baked up more cookies and treats then the family needed for a year. Oh, yeah, something was up. And they weren't telling me a thing.

I quickly learned that Malcolm's family was more than fun and games. In fact, there hadn't been much joking since that first breakfast together. Who knew what went on after I collapsed on my bed at night? They probably sharpened their collection of knives hidden away in some secret closet or they practiced torture techniques using kitchen tools. But I couldn't complain. They kept their end of the bargain. My family was safe. I was safe. And Constance was safe. No poison in the whole-wheat pancakes Will offered one morning. And I was being trained to protect myself.

The weekend finally came. The whole family went out for dinner. Even though they were gone, it took quite a bit of pacing outside Bartholomew's office to gather the courage to even open the door. The afternoon light was fast fading, and I wanted to get inside before I'd have to use a flashlight. Even though I hadn't seen evidence of henchman, I suspected that was due to their skill in keeping with the shadows. They were sure to suspect a bobbing light inside the most important room in the house, and I didn't want to find out what they'd do to intruders. Even if I was a houseguest.

With a hand on the knob, I listened to the quiet. It was unnerving not hearing Edith complain or the pans rattling in the kitchen or Bartholomew's booming voice. But this was my time. I might not get another chance.

I gripped the doorknob and opened the heavy oak door. The moon shining through the glass doors that opened into the garden spotlighted Bartholomew's desk. What was I looking for? A file or a locked cabinet? A photo? Something. But they were too smart to leave evidence lying around. I ran my fingers around the bottom of his desk in search of a lever. I opened his desk drawers but found nothing but office supplies. There was nothing but damn office supplies.

At first, the office seemed like a real place to work: the desk, a photo, office supplies like Staples was a candy store. But something was missing. Other than the family photo there was nothing personal. Like the set up could be in an office decor magazine. They were one step ahead of me. This was a fake office.

So where was the real one? The one with all the hidden papers and scribbled notes that revealed their nasty plans for Constance. I might've left my mom behind but I liked to think about it as more of an undercover role. I mean, yes, I was training in exchange for safety but this wouldn't last forever. At some point the sweet cookie would crumble and we'd go back to being mortal enemies.

Before that happened, before I left, probably running for my life with a family of assassins hot on my trail, I'd find some info on their plans.

I circled the desk and went straight to the fireplace and the panels next to it. I pressed, pushed, pulled.

Nothing.

I ran my fingers along the edges where the panel met the wall, searching for some kind of button or oddly shaped lever. Nothing. I faced the wall and studied every oddly colored brick and grouting around the fireplace.

Something nudged the back of my legs and I jumped.

"Prince!" I rubbed the top of his head as my pulse relaxed. "You scared the crap out of me."

He tilted his head and looked at me as if puzzled, questioning my decision to spy on his owners.

"You don't get it, Prince. It's complicated and I don't have enough time to explain. But, someday, you and me, we'll take a long walk along the seashore and I'll tell you every bit of my complicated life."

He flopped to the floor, his large head resting on his paws, and watched me. I moved my attention from the panels to the fireplace. Yes, I went back to my Nancy Drew days. The bricks felt rough under my fingers but I felt each and every one, pressing and pushing. Until I heard a slight click and a door slid open to the right of the fireplace. I sucked in my breath. I was in.

After several glances toward the door and peeks out the window to assure myself the family had not returned, I flicked on my mini flashlight. It barely penetrated the blackness, and I crept inside, with Prince at my heels. I pulled on the string, which turned on a naked bulb hanging from the ceiling. It was a little disappointing. I didn't know what I expected but the room was kinda boring. Filing cabinets. And more filing cabinets. A couple of chairs and a small table. That was it. I'd been hoping for an open file labeled Constance. Not happening.

Prince growled as if warning me to leave. My neck prickled as I slid open the first cabinet. I flipped through the files until I found the G section. And sure enough, the first one was Constance Gerald. Hungry for knowledge on him, I opened it right there.

My eyes widened. The file held every little factoid about his life: birth date, address, weight, height, and eye color. It ran down a list of addresses he'd called home. A date was highlighted in yellow so I ran my finger along the date line. Seemed he came into quite a bit of money a few years ago, quit his job and purchased his current home. Interesting.

One name caught my eye. It was scribbled underneath the highlighting.

Robert Yertsky.

I searched the rest of the file but there was no explanation of his connection to Constance or Will's family plans on assassinating Constance. Prince barked and jogged from the room. I took that as my sign to go. They were too smart to leave the details of their future crime in the folder in the secret room. I slipped out and pressed the same brick for the door to slide shut. I'd go back to my room and read. I didn't need to tiptoe but for some reason I couldn't help it. Maybe all my midnight trips to gorge on lemon bars had created a bad habit. I flicked the light on in the kitchen. How much time had I spent in the secret room?

"Good evening, Savvy." Bartholomew stood behind the kitchen counter. His greeting wasn't the friendly kind of good evening. More like a Darth Vader kind of greeting.

I froze mid-creep, the blood draining from my face and the feeling of ultimate doom flushing my body. Damn. I was losing my touch.

Nineteen

BARTHOLOMEW POINTED TO A chair against the wall. I stumbled over to it, wondering if I should make a break for it. Janelle and Edith gathered around him with stony faces and hands clasped. A plate of lemon bars lay on the kitchen bar.

Edith focused on me with a sickly sweet smile. A heat rash spread like wildfire across my neck. My mouth went instantly dry and I stuck my hands under my legs to hide the trembling. Every few seconds I glanced at the hall, hoping Malcolm would enter.

"Would you like a lemon bar, Savvy?" Edith rubbed her fingers over the top of her cane. "We know how much you like them."

"Um, no thanks. I'll pass," I said a little too quickly, my words sounding breathy. From my shaky words to my trembling fingers, I might as well plead guilty. Did they know what I'd been up to? Infiltrating their secret files?

Edith spoke. "No really. We know you're dying to."

Janelle hid her smile.

"Hush." Bartholomew scolded but I saw the corners of his mouth turn up. He cleared his throat and straightened his back. Any humor left his expression, and his eyebrows drew together and his lips pressed into a straight line.

Edith cleared her throat in a loud and intentional way. "Savvy, you are on trial for stealing lemon bars."

I glanced at the steel in Edith's eyes, and the firm set of Bartholomew's jaw. Sweat broke out on my forehead. I prayed to the spy gods they didn't know I'd broken into his secret room.

"That's right you should be scared," Edith stated.

Bartholomew coughed. "I'm the judge. I'll make the comments."

But Edith wasn't done. "You should just thank your lucky lemon bars that Will wasn't a part of our plan. He'd have sliced your throat in the middle of the night without blinking an eye. No questions asked."

I swallowed down fear but it lodged in my throat. My eyes darted between all of them, searching for a bit of empathy, but my gaze slammed up against a stone cold wall.

"Squirm away," Edith said with a grin like the Cheshire cat. "Last week, lemon bars were missing and the remaining ones carefully rearranged. There's only one person in this house who eats lemon bars."

"And that's Edith," Bartholomew stated.

Edith gave me a rather pointed look with a disapproving scowl. "No one else eats lemon bars without my permission. Especially company."

"What did you expect?" My words were clipped as anger overtook my fear. "I've been eating nothing but raw grains and veggies." Seriously. I was almost one hundred percent positive that if I'd been allowed some normal food, like cupcakes or cookies, I wouldn't have even glanced at the lemon bars. Or, at least, only taken a bite.

Bartholomew nodded. "We can understand to a certain degree. But rules are rules."

"Enough with the lemon bars." Edith narrowed her eyes. "Anything else you'd like to admit to?"

This was a trap. I knew it. And maybe if I threw myself at their feet and begged for mercy, they'd let me off with a warning. But I couldn't do it. The stubborn side rose up, the part that resented their family and their role in my family not being together and happy. "No."

"Wrong answer. Continue, Bartholomew."

"Last week Edith devised a plan. A time when we'd leave you in the house alone. A test you might say." He shook his head. "And sadly, you didn't pass. You were just sneaking out of my office," Bartholomew said, directing his comment to me. "And that is the only piece of evidence needed to conclude your guilt."

"No one enters the secret room," Edith said, her eyes flashing victory as if she loved this moment of going in for the kill and humiliating me.

"Very true." Janelle shook her head and kept her eyes down, focusing on the patterns in the granite countertop.

Bartholomew stood and paced. "Instead of executing you on the spot and dumping your body in the Mediterranean, we've decided to up the mission you must perform in exchange for your stay with us. An addendum to the contract between you and Will. Honey?"

Janelle took over. "Now there are two missions you must complete. Edith?"

She rapped her cane against the floor in final judgment. "And we've moved up the date. Tomorrow, your training ends and your mission begins." Her voice sounded like tiny rock fragments blocked her throat. "And no more lemon bars."

The hope in my chest wilted and the prickles of fear reached down and encircled my heart, making it extremely hard to breathe. How could I not have seen their set up? The devious way in which Bartholomew let it slip a few days ago that they were going out for an evening. I fell for it like a complete sucker. Somehow I didn't feel anywhere close to ready for any kind of mission they might throw at me. Crap. What had I done?

The next morning I awoke after a terrible night spent tossing and turning. I pulled the pillow over my head, trying to ignore the growing pit in my stomach and the fear that over time I'd become one of them. A part of me regretted not running away with Malcolm when I had the chance.

"Good morning!" Janelle chirped as she burst through the door.

I sensed the flash of light as she opened my shade. I groaned and pulled the pillow over my head.

"Figures," said Edith. "We bring her breakfast in bed and she complains. I knew it. Ingrate."

"Huh?" I scrambled to the surface and threw my pillow aside. A T.V. tray stood next to my bed with several plates of food. Blueberry pancakes drizzled with syrup. Scrambled eggs. Bacon. Orange juice and hot chocolate. I got lost in the swirling steam.

"I don't get it. What happened to unsweetened oatmeal and apple slices?"

A big smile spread across Janelle's face. "Your first mission is this afternoon. Training is over."

I squinted at the sunlight, my eyes still not adjusted. "Did you run this past Will? I mean, I haven't seen him in a while."

"Will, schmill," Edith stated. "He's not God's gift as he thinks."

"Oh, shush," Janelle said, glancing around as if Will was listening. "Our family wouldn't be what it is without him. Don't forget that."

Edith snorted. "I can't forget it. He reminds me all the time."

Janelle focused on me. "Will arrived early this morning. He's just fine with it."

Will? Was home? Any safety I'd felt with this family dissolved. Had he left behind a trail of dead bodies on his travels? I sank my fork into the pancakes, forcing my appetite back. "Thank you."

"Well, dear. It's a tradition." She hummed as she laid out several fancy sundresses for me to wear.

"Yeah, tradition all right," Edith said. "The one in the most danger gets the biggest breakfast because it could be their last."

I choked on a piece of bacon.

After breakfast Janelle fussed over me like I was her daughter attending prom. I couldn't even remember the last time my mom brought me breakfast in bed or called me pretty.

"What's wrong, dear?" Janelle ran a brush through my hair. "You seem sad."

I plastered on a smile. "I'm fine."

I pushed those sad feelings back where they belonged in my secret hidden place I'd developed since living with them. I was getting pretty good at this and that scared me the most.

"Why don't you try on the dresses and we'll see which one fits best."

"The bra. Give her bra." The cane tapped on the floor.

A bra?

"That's right," Edith said. "Women need to use their God-given tools to distract their enemy. It could save your life."

Somehow I couldn't quite imagine that but I didn't argue. I spent the next hour or so trying on dresses. It was a delicate balance between what looked best on me but wouldn't attract too much attention. My secret mission was to remain a secret. Even from me.

Twenty

AFTER WE SETTLED ON a dress, a long gorgeous number that swirled down near my calves, made of a sheeny sparkly blue material, we moved on to my hair.

"What do you think, Edith?" Janelle asked. "The hot rollers or up?"

"Definitely up. Show off that gorgeous neck and bring out her eyes."

Janelle made me sit on the bed. She plunked down a huge bag filled with clips, pins, barrettes and combs. Tirelessly, she twisted, primped, pruned, clipped and pinned. Then she moved on to the make-up.

"This is my specialty, dear. I can still send Bartholomew into a tizzy with the right balance of eye shadow and lipstick."

As Janelle tweezed and brushed, I dreaded looking in the mirror. What if I looked like a clown?

"Step on it, Janelle. We have lots more to cover than make-up."

"Okay, okay, I'm done." She pulled out a mirror.

I gasped. That was me? The elegant, beautiful girl, no woman, with sparkles tinting her eyelids and cheekbones. I didn't recognize the person I was turning into. Dad would be so proud. He'd want to waltz me around the room while Mom took pictures. At least in my fantasies. "Wow, you are good."

Edith waved off my remark. "Don't build her ego up more than it already it is."

We moved into the sunroom next. They ran down a list of dos and don'ts about buffet manners and eating. I shouldn't eat too much but I should eat something. Make sure to have a drink in my hand so I could either beg off to go to the bathroom or accidentally spill it if I needed a quick exit. Try to stay invisible. Flit around the room, nod, say hello, agree with conversation. Do just enough so that I fit in but not enough that people remember me.

"Maybe you should tell me about the mission now?" I suggested as nicely as I could.

"Sorry, dear. I talked with Will this morning. You won't know anything until minutes before."

"But, but, I need to be prepared!" How could I form some kind of plan without knowing the details?

"Ha!" The word burst from Edith's mouth. "You lost that privilege when you violated our trust."

"Oh." The mirage of this whole dress-up day faded. I couldn't forget that this family, these women were my mortal enemies. They were dressing me up to send me out, without a concern in the world. They didn't care about me. At all.

"We might've told you, dear, but we can't risk you leaving and telling your mother. We don't want to put you in the position of choosing us over your mother. And we really don't want to kill you."

"Speak for yourself," Edith said.

"Oh, shush. Stop being so insensitive."

They reminded me a little bit of Adamos in that I couldn't pull anything over on him. I stayed lost in my thoughts about what lay ahead of me. I didn't know which was worse: knowing or not knowing.

"Dancing!" Edith rapped her cane on the floor.

Janelle pressed both hands to the sides of her face. "Oh my, how could we forget about the dancing!"

"Dancing?" I asked. "I thought this was an afternoon tea?"

Janelle rushed about the room, pulling furniture to the right and left to leave space. "Yes, but the host loves to dance. Often at his luncheons, he'll have a dance or two. You must know at least the waltz."

"Your mom didn't happen to teach you any moves on the floor along with how to spy, did she?" asked Edith.

"No. Mom didn't teach me anything." The words slipped out with the emotion attached before I could stop them.

A tense silence followed my admission, until Edith spoke. "That's just like a spy, cold and heartless. Not surprised at all."

Janelle fumbled with the CDs. "All I can find are Bartholomew's old Harry Chapin music. That won't do at all."

"I can hum," Edith said, settling into her chair for a show.

"It'll have to do." Janelle took my hands and wrapped one hand around my waist and held the other. She tried counting and leading but kept stepping on my toes. "I'm sorry. I'm not used to this. Too bad Malcolm isn't here. He's the best dancer out of all of us."

"What are you saying about me?" Malcolm said, striding into the room.

The air around him seemed charged with electricity. He walked with a swagger, his shoulders straighter. In the days since Will had left on business, Malcolm had grown into a new person, more confident and comfortable with his family. And despite the fact that we weren't together right now and maybe not forever, I smiled.

Janelle clapped her hands together. "Perfect timing." She stepped aside and swept her arm out as if presenting me for his approval.

His eyes narrowed as he studied my face and then they dropped to my body. They swept down the low-cut front, the material that hugged my waist and the flowing bodice. "She'll do."

A slight shiver traveled down the length of my back. His dark jeans and white button-up shirt complimented his hair and reflected his dark eyes. My heart flip-flopped. A slight flush spread across my cheeks, and he tilted his head and smirked.

Malcolm connected his iPod to a dock. "Really, Mother. You must catch up on the latest technology."

"I know plenty."

He laughed. "Knowing how to load and operate a bazooka doesn't count."

And with that the music started. His hand pressed against the small of my back and he clasped my hand in his. Tingles shot through my fingers and spread across my skin. I swayed forward and breathed in his scent, wishing we were on a date and not preparing for a spy mission. He led me around the room, the music matching our steps. I tried not to step on his toes or bang into shins.

"Relax," he whispered. "Just follow my lead."

"I can't dance!" I hissed in his ear.

"You'll do just fine." He smiled while keeping his head in the correct position.

Malcolm swept me around the floor and after the first few times I got the hang of it. Either that or he led extremely well. The music stopped and Malcolm hesitated before pulling away. His eyes rested on mine, and a window opened to his soul. For a brief moment, the emotions that he kept so tightly guarded showed. I saw the real Malcolm, the boy, the man, vulnerable and open, the one who wasn't the assassin. He cared about me, regardless of what he said about being friends.

"How'd I do?" I whispered.

He didn't answer, his hand still clasped in mine. The next song started and he led me around the floor again. My dress swirled around my legs, the air kissed my heated face, and Malcolm pulled me closer to him. His heart beat through his shirt and against my chest. The music rose to a crescendo and then dropped. Malcolm dipped me, his face inches from mine and I got lost in the charcoal flecks in his eyes.

"Is she ready?" Will's question permeated the room, sending an icy dagger between Malcolm and me.

Malcolm whipped me back up and squeezed my hand. "She's ready."

Will strode forward and sized me up, his face and body language emanating disapproval, then he focused on his brother. "I'll need you to take her to the luncheon. I need to report to father. Can you handle that little brother? Without messing up?"

Malcolm saluted in mock submission. "Sure thing, bro."

And my heart skipped with joy.

Twenty-one

MALCOLM AND I ARRIVED at the afternoon tea. All I could say was afternoon tea my ass. Afternoon teas don't have an orchestra the size of my hometown in Pennsylvania or one hundred waiters circling with platters of food, or ice sculptures decorating the lawn. Seriously.

"I thought this was a tea?" I whispered as Malcolm led me down the bluestone walkway.

"You don't run in the right circles. Trust me, this is nothing."

Hmpf. What did he think? I was some sort of highfalutin' southern belle with myriads of friends in high places? Hardly. And he knew it. He knew my history down to the size of my underwear and that I liked rainbow fuzzy socks instead of cotton anklets. I was sure his family knew more about me than I knew about myself.

A waiter came by serving champagne. I was about to decline, but then remembered Janelle's advice about always having a drink in my hand and not eating too much. I held onto the glass like it was my best friend, pretending to sip it.

Many different groups of people approached Malcolm. He clearly was the man to know. Men spoke in low voices to him. Older women pinched his cheeks and chatted about Edith. Young women floated by, wiggling their hips and casting me haughty looks and then smiling as soon as Malcolm turned his attention on them.

I smiled and nodded, not engaging in too much conversation while scouting the place. I might not know my mission but I'd be prepared. I found potential hiding places behind sculpted hedges. I found a weapon in the sword on an ice sculpture. I found two different exits: through the main driveway and out through a break in the hedges on the side lawn. There were two main entrances to the house/mansion—one through magnificent French doors and another on the side where the waiters kept flooding out with more food.

Next I observed the guests. They all kinda blurred together, the men in their tuxes and the women in their fancy dresses and cloying perfume. At one point, I managed to catch Malcolm during a pause between the flocks of people that were drawn to him.

"You certainly are popular," I said into his ear.

He looked at me with an odd expression, one of surprise and admiration mixed together. "You really have no idea, do you?"

"About what?" Panic seized my stomach and I glanced around. Were there terrorists surrounding me? Were the waiters really monks in disguise and I didn't know it? "Tell me."

He stepped close so his lips brushed my ear. "How beautiful you are."

"Yeah, right." I laughed almost snorting out the tiny sip of champagne I'd taken.

"Especially when you're just being you." Malcolm leaned close once again. "They're flocking to me, to get a closer look at you."

I had a hard time believing that so as the heat burned in my cheeks, I babbled out some words, trying to make light of it. "So much for blending into the crowd."

"Mother did much too good a job with you."

He suddenly stiffened and gripped my arm as an older attractive man with black wavy hair strode toward us. He held his head high and the arrogant look in his eyes told me this man was used to getting what he wanted. The orchestra started a slow number and my fingers tapped the rhythm of the waltz. Malcolm's hold on my arm grew tighter.

"You're hurting me."

Malcolm's smile grew, but I recognized it as fake, a total act.

The man stuck out his hand. "Dear friend, how nice of you to come. And who is this lovely woman by your side?"

Instantly the man gave me the creeps, the way he made sure our eyes made direct contact, the way he touched my arm as he shook hands with Malcolm, the way he smiled while talking, which looked totally stupid. Sometimes, a girl has to follow her instinct and mine was telling me that this guy was no good.

"Come now, introduce us before I lose my chance to spin her across the dance floor."

"Actually, she and I were just heading in that direction."

Malcolm moved his hand to my lower back and pushed me forward, leaving the creepo in the dust. Once on the floor, he took the lead and we moved as one. Kinda. More like he didn't grimace when I took the wrong step or moved in the wrong direction.

"Who was that?" Malcolm's gaze flicked back and forth between the crowds and me. "Hey! Who's the creep?" I repeated.

"Shh. Just dance." Malcolm spun me, my skirt swirling.

When the waltz ended, he kept me close and moved into another slow dance as the orchestra stayed with the same pace. He placed his cheek against mine, his breathing a bit faster than usual.

I felt safe, which was nice. Then he spoke, shattering any pretense of a lovely afternoon tea.

"That man was Robert Yertsky, friend of Constance. He's one of the most dangerous men in the country. For some reason, he set his sight on you."

"Ew. He's way too old," I said jokingly, but the name struck a chord. His name had been on Constance's file in the secret room. What was their connection?

"That doesn't matter to someone like him. This will make your mission even harder. Understand? It's imperative you don't waste time. When I leave, enter the house immediately, find his office and take pictures of anything on his desk, anything suspicious or personal."

Malcolm paused as a couple moved within hearing range. He traced his hand down my back and kissed the soft skin near my ear. His hips swayed against mine as he pressed me closer. He steered me away and withdrew, leaving me a little bit breathless.

I tried to get the words out. "But what if—"

"There are no what ifs. You get in, you get out. I'll be waiting down the street in the car."

I grabbed the sleeve of his tux. "But why just pictures? Is someone going to swoop in after me and do the real work?" I made the slight motion of drawing my hand across my neck.

Malcolm pressed his lips together. "Robert hired us to take care of Constance and we're investigating both sides."

I mouthed the word "Oh" and winked at him. "Gotcha."

I took advantage of the precious few seconds before he'd leave me. I walked my fingers up his chest. "You know, just in case I die or something, could you tell me anything about my mom?"

Malcolm turned his back to another couple and slowly moved us closer to the entrance of the house. "From the little I know, your mom and Will have dealt with each other in the past, but if she hasn't told you about their relationship, then I doubt Will would either."

His words and the little bit of truth they contained lingered, and I couldn't shake them off. Mom knew Will? Personally? Had she struck some kind of deal with him too? At that point, we'd reached the end of the dance floor. He spun me once more. His hand brushed across the top of the exposed skin of my chest—thanks to the miracle bra.

"There is a miniature camera on the inside of your bra. I just dropped it into a tiny pocket. Take as many pictures of papers or anything you can find on Constance. Good luck."

Then he turned and walked away, disappearing into the crowd.

I stood alone, my body still tingling from his touch and the insta-fear his words had produced. Go inside. Find office. Take pictures. Leave.

Simple.

Simple until creepo spotted and bee lined toward me.

Twenty-two

I FROZE AS ROBERT walked toward me with a smug grin, each step filled with purpose. Three older gentlemen with arrogance in their stride, all carrying their brandies, passed in front of him. I took the opportunity to dash behind the nearest art sculpture, realized that was a terrible idea, and then dove behind the hedge decorating the side of the house. I crouched, the fringes of my dress skimming the neatly trimmed lawn. I wanted to stay right there and wish this whole thing away.

Robert spun slowly in a circle, his eagle eyes searching every face on the dance floor. He craned his neck and I prayed the guy would pull a muscle. His false sense of power rolled off him in waves. As guests passed him they tried to sneak in a word or two with him but he brushed them off. At one point, his gaze rested on the hedge and I immediately came up with some excuses as to why I was crouched there. I dropped an earring. I had a panic/anxiety disorder. I thought he was the biggest creep and was avoiding him. Okay that one probably wouldn't go over too well but I was beginning to appreciate the truth since it was something I barely experienced.

Luck intervened and a slutty blonde sidled up to him, her chest pushed out and brushing his suit coat. His gaze naturally travelled downward and then she grabbed his arm and led him to the dance floor. Thankfully, the creep couldn't say no to beauty. As soon as he turned his back, I dashed into the front entrance.

Inside, while my eyes adjusted to the dark, I rubbed my arms. I could do this. Get in and get out. No problem. Voices of waiters neared and I snuck into a hallway and pressed up against the wall. As soon as they passed I followed Malcolm's instructions: straight through the first room, down the stair, first hallway on the right, second door on the left.

The door opened easily and I slipped inside. The large office was nothing like Bartholomew's and at first I couldn't move. Pottery was smashed on the floor, their shards in scattered piles. Intricately designed wrought iron lamps lay across one another like a pile of Pick Up Sticks. The entire room seemed a mishmash of different cultures from the thick Persian rug to the pottery to the odds and ends stacked on shelves. Had someone searched the room before me? My heart plummeted as I realized the evidence I needed to photograph might have been stolen.

The whole creep vibe pulsed in the room and freaked me out. I went straight to the desk, which had papers piled up just waiting for me. I fumbled inside my dress for the mini camera and started taking random pictures of the papers on the desk. One after another. This took several minutes and then I went to the first filing cabinet. I searched for Gerald and pulled out his file. I snapped more pictures, but I had a feeling this was the same background information we already had on Constance.

But I noticed a map, hand drawn blueprints of some kind of building but there were huge chunks missing. The ends were torn as if he studied this a lot. My fingers tingled just touching the worn paper. With a delicate touch, I folded it and stuck it inside the secret compartment of the purse Janelle had loaned me, then I stuffed the file back in the cabinet.

I moved onto the wooden crate against the wall that should've been in a warehouse and not a plush office. With my fingertips under the lid, I pulled it up. Dusty scrolls and parchments were stacked to the brim.

"Find anything interesting?"

I dropped the lid with a slam and whipped around to find Robert leaning against the doorway, with a predatory grin.

"I, um, was looking for the bathroom," I blurted out. Crap.

"Bathroom, really." He massaged the sides of his chin. "I find that rather odd."

I took a few steps toward the doorway, but he moved to block my exit.

"Why would a pretty little thing like yourself in need of a tinkle look for a bathroom on the basement floor. Why not on the first floor? Why not ask one of the waiters?"

"They were occupied, and you know, I had to go." I crossed my legs for effect.

"Hmm." He rested his hand on a lamp and then two seconds later sent it crashing to the floor, the bulb shattering and tiny pieces of glass scattering. "I don't like it when people lie to me."

Needle pricks of panic started in my toes and spread up my legs until they attacked my chest. I could barely breathe. I realized that the damage in the room was the result of his uncontrollable rage. He made up the distance between us in three giant strides. Within seconds, the sudden rage passed and lust took its place. His eyes moved from my face and then lower, desire flashing as he wiggled his fingers in anticipation.

It was all I could do not to spit in his face. I leaned one arm against the wall and struck a casual pose like a proper spy in a moment of danger, but then he let the backs of his fingers trail down the side of my arm.

"You might need to be punished for trespassing."

All my training seeped out of my mind and lay in a puddle on the floor. The tips, the advice, the knowledge abandoned me.

"People always misunderstand me." Again, the rage flickered in the pulsing of his jaw. He grabbed a ceramic mug from the desk and smashed it against the wall. Then his twitching muscles calmed and he said casually, "They say I have a temper."

I winced.

"But really, I don't. It's quite simple. If people respect me, I respect them." His hand moved up and into my hair and he pulled me toward him. His whiskey breath blasted my face, the sour smell making my insides curl. "Why, why, why, do people think they can cross me?"

"Because they're stupid?" I closed my eyes, to prevent a tear from leaking out the side.

He yanked my head back. Pain rippled across my scalp and I hung in midair. He controlled my body like my hair strands were strings and I was the puppet. He yanked me back up and brought his mouth to my ear. "Smart girl."

He threw me to the ground and I gasped as the wind got knocked out of me. I scrambled away from him on all fours.

"Come now. No need to be so scared." He jumped with ease and sat on his desk. "It's really rather simple. You tell me why you're here and then I'll see if I can help you. If I can't, I'll let you go."

"What?"

"You heard me and I'm a man of my word." He snorted. "Unlike some I know."

I struggled for words. I couldn't tell him about the pictures but I could feed him half-truths. "The family I'm living with, they sent me." Doubt flickered on his face so I smiled like I was telling the truth when in fact I had no idea why they'd sent me into this man's house or why they wanted pictures of his private papers.

"Ah, yes. I know exactly the family you're referring to. That doesn't surprise me at all, the bumbling amateurs. But that's not your fault and I consider myself a fair man." He tapped his chin. "Now why would they send an amateur like you to spy on me when they are more than capable of taking care of the job? And what could they possibly need that I haven't already told them? Hmm. How fun!" He clapped in excitement. "I do like a good puzzle." He was back at my side before I could move. He traced his hand down my jaw and lingered right below my mouth. "And you my dear are an interesting one."

"They want to know about Constance," I blurted out, anxious to get as far away from this man as possible. No wonder Will's family wanted to spy on this guy: they didn't trust him. I wouldn't either and I didn't need assassin instincts to figure that out.

Robert didn't have a quick reply at the ready. The name Constance seemed to affect him. His face paled but slowly turned various shades of red from the neck up. He fiddled with a pencil and snapped it in half.

"That traitor!" His words shot out, laced with venom and hatred. He paced the room, mumbling to himself.

I inched toward the door, ready to run and never look back. Malcolm was telling the truth: Robert was mad at Constance and hired assassins to do away with him. I hid my gasp.

He flipped and marched toward me. "I already told them everything about that traitor!" His fingers wrapped around my bare arms and he shook me. "Why are you really here?" He let go and beat his chest with his fist. "To kill me?"

"No, absolutely not. I, I don't know anything."

"Ha! Liar!" He patted my head and seemed to calm down with every stroke of my hair. "That's okay, I'll tell you even if they won't. Constance is a thief!" He pointed a finger in the air and his face reddened again. "We were partners! Then he bowed out, after stealing the map and handing me a fake. You hear me? He took my money and never followed through! Cutting me out of everything. My hopes. My dreams. That kind of betrayal only deserves one kind of punishment."

He didn't have to tell me. "Death?"

Robert's anger disappeared again, and he did another one eighty, transforming back into the smiling host. "Too bad you got caught with your fingers in the cookie jar. You've told me the truth, what you know of it. I can see you're just a pawn." He struck a finger in the air. "But," his voice got louder, "even pawns must pay their dues."

Robert came at me with his hands aimed at my boobs.

Twenty-three

HIS HANDS BRIEFLY SKIMMED my chest and light twinkled in his eyes, then the lunatic grasped my hand and dragged me to the middle of the office floor. I struggled, but his iron grip made it impossible to escape.

"We never did get our dance. That naughty boy kept you all to himself."

My cheeks flamed.

"You are quite transparent. One dance with me, and you'll forget all about him. The ladies simply can't resist me."

He clapped and music flicked on to some sort of waltz. He put one arm behind my back and held the other one up in the air. "May I have this dance?"

"Do I have a choice?"

"Ooh, I like a girl with some spice. You could say no…"

His words trailed off but I didn't care for the underlying suggestion of what would happen if I did say no, so I played along. He wasn't nearly as good as Malcolm and I felt stiff and awkward.

"Relax," he whispered in my ear as his hand rubbed my lower back and slid down to my butt.

I wanted to puke and kick some major bad guy ass. But I had to be smart. I'd seen enough movies to know to play along until the right time, after he'd fallen under my seductive spell and relaxed.

He twirled me under his arm and then resumed the position. "I'm willing to forgive and forget, but your boss needs to realize he can't mess with me."

Robert continued to talk but it was mostly egotistical babble. I flashed back to all the training in the past few weeks, the impromptu running and fights and missions through Athens. This was what I'd prepared for, a moment like this, filled with danger, a bad guy, and me. My patience with waiting for the right moment wore thin. I wasn't doing anything but letting this guy control the situation. Major spy fail moment. I jerked out of my thoughts when he pushed me away. In a blur I saw his hand pull back but I didn't understand what was happening until I felt the sting of his hand on my face. Tears sprang to my eyes.

He yanked me close again. "When I talk people listen and you are no exception. Understand?"

I nodded, numb with the shock and pain of his action. He resumed the dancing position and forced me across the floor. I stumbled and found it hard to keep up the pretense. I was done being the stooge, the 'fraidy cat. I'd subjected myself to Will and his family and the dangers that came with that so I'd be able to defend myself. I certainly didn't risk it all for nothing, for this.

I kicked him in the shins and then ducked. "Sorry. Guess I'm a bit clueless."

Robert grabbed his leg. His eyes flashed. "That wasn't very nice." He reached out to grab a fistful of hair but I swerved.

Malcolm's words came back to me. Use what you have. You might not always have a gun or knife on you. And wasn't that the truth? I peeled my feet off the floor and took a step toward the back wall. I just happened to pick up a letter opener on the way. Robert growled and moved toward me slowly. I held up my fists, the sharp end of the file pointing out.

"Don't think I won't take you out," I threatened.

He laughed. "Oh, my dear. You are such a treat, a breath of fresh air. No wonder those silly assassins keep you around. What fun." In response to my brandishing a file, he undid the belt from around his waist and snapped it in the air.

Prickles popped. My heart pumped blood so hard and fast it sounded like a base drum. I dropped the letter opener and dove for his legs, hoping to knock him over. He fell but then I took a foot in the side of the head. With my ears ringing and blurred vision I attacked again with my fists, ready to pound his face, but I missed. He moved with the poise of a ninja and it became clear that this psycho had many more weeks, probably years, of training than me.

I grabbed a pottery shard and threw it at his head. It spun and wobbled through the air and even though he saw it coming he didn't dodge it fast enough. My lucky day. The edge scraped his cheek and created a three-inch gash. Blood flowed instantly and dripped down his face. A few spots landed on his fancy clothes. He lifted his fingers up and pulled them away. His eyes widened and his face slowly turned color, matching the dark red that stained his cheek.

"This new suit just arrived from Paris." His words spit out from between his clenched teeth. "The games are over, honey. You want to dance with the big boys?"

"Bring it on!" I yelled, though I couldn't hide the tremor in my voice.

He charged at me though without the belt. Instead he used his body force and rammed me into the wall. Breath shot out from my chest and I crumpled to the floor, sucking in air. He kicked me in the stomach and as soon as I stumbled to my feet, he punched my back and pushed me into the desk. The side of my face hit a vase and cracked the glass in two.

He laughed.

I slumped across the desk. My cheek rested on the cool metal. Pain shot through my body and I could barely move. I groaned, making sure he could hear, hoping to lure him closer. His mocking chuckles pushed me to slide my hand across the desk and grasp a paperweight.

"Oh, dear. I hope your family of assassins don't mind that I play with the new intern." He traced a finger down my back and handled my butt. Again.

Too far, man. Way too far.

He pressed his hips up against my backside and stretched his body over mine. He nibbled my ear. "I think some punishment is in order."

My fingers dug into the paperweight and as soon as creepo gave me wriggle room, I flipped and brought the weight against his head. He slumped over onto me and we crashed to the floor. My chest heaved and I gasped for breath under his weight. I couldn't talk. I couldn't think. I couldn't move. But I was alive.

Someone knocked on the door and yelled, "Savvy!"

I groaned, but Malcolm couldn't hear me. I think it was Malcolm. It sounded like Malcolm.

"The door is locked. Open it up!"

"Okay." My voice quivered. I put my hands against Robert's meaty body and pushed with all my strength. Finally with one last grunt and hard shove, he rolled off. I crawled across the floor and reached up and unlocked the door. Malcolm opened it just as I fell forward.

Mission accomplished. And I was alive.

His strong arms around me had never felt so good. My head fell against his shirt, and his smell, his warmth embraced me. He pulled away. His eyes filled with love and concern, he touched the cut on my cheek. "What did that asshole do?"

"I'll tell you later." I grabbed his hand, ready to collapse.

He kissed my forehead and then we ran. The halls flashed by. Smells of freshly baked bread assaulted me. The kitchen. Cooks gasped. Malcolm spoke in Greek and soothed their concerns. Then fresh air brushed my skin, creating goosebumps.

I passed out from exhaustion right near the car. He lay me down in the backseat. Smoothing my hair against my face. Whispering in my ear. Kissing my cheek. Making promises.

But promises didn't mean anything to me. Not anymore.

Twenty-four

"MALCOLM?" I MURMURED.

"Shh," he said into my ear. "Don't talk. We're on my boat."

My cheek throbbed. I lifted my hand to touch it but Malcolm caught my fingers in his hand. "Don't touch it. Let me clean it up first."

"Why?" I asked.

"Why what?" He lowered me to the floor with one arm behind my back.

"Why me?" Last year I put off college and went to Paris with my dad. He started Spy Games and we made due. And then Malcolm entered my life and it hadn't been the same since. "What if we'd never met? Would I still be in Paris with my dad, living blissfully unaware?"

He dabbed at the cut on my cheek with a washcloth and then dipped it into a bowl of hot water, rinsing between each dab and dunk.

"I don't think you'd be blissfully unaware. You'd be unhappy and doing anything you could to find answers. Here, today, you might not like the answers you found, but you found them."

I couldn't argue with that. I eyed the small kit he pulled out from a chest/bench.

"This gash would probably heal on its own but I don't want to chance it. You might have a scar." He tenderly touched my skin, then rubbed numbing gel across it. Gently, he placed a butterfly Band-Aid on it. "That should do it."

His hands ran across my shoulders. I shivered when he unzipped my dress and the cool metal ran down my back.

I pushed up even though my body cried out. "Hey!"

"Savvy, come on. This has nothing to do with you and me. This has to do with taking care of you. Let me?"

I sank back down and nodded.

"Be right back." He kissed my forehead, and then disappeared into the bathroom.

Wincing, I slid my dress off and wrapped up in it doing the best I could to keep the important parts covered. The steam escaped from his small bathroom, the shower running at full strength. He helped me into the room.

"I got it from here," I said.

"Okay. Call me if you need anything. I'll try and find some food but I'm not promising anything." Then he left and shut the door.

I stepped into the stream of hot water and tried to scrub off the memories of the last twelve hours. Back in his room, I changed into his T-shirt and sweats then searched my spy bra for the camera.

It wasn't there. I fought the rush of panic. That was the whole point of my scuffle with Robert.

I grabbed the dress from the floor and shook it out, hoping a small black camera would fall. It didn't. I fell to my hands and knees and searched the floor, under the bed, in every corner. After running my hands over every inch of the floor, I slumped against the bed.

I'd failed my mission.

Later, I curled up next to him on his bed with a platter of crackers, cheese and beer in front of us. We munched in silence or more like devoured.

"You're not eating," I said between bites.

"I've trained under my brother before. I assume you're half starved."

I nodded. "Totally."

We fell silent. I sipped the beer, letting it numb me a little bit from the inside out. I dreaded talking about anything significant, all the matters that weighed down on us from the outside in.

Right after finishing up the food, Malcolm pulled me closer. "Why don't you sleep? We'll talk tomorrow."

I didn't complain and tried to sleep, snug in his arms. Flashbacks of Robert's twisted, evil face and the feel of his hands on me kept me awake. My body ached where'd he'd used me for boxing practice. Finally, I drifted off. The last thing I remembered was Malcolm kissing the side of my head and whispering, "We need to keep you out of danger."

Every time I woke, the sunlight fell farther and deeper into the cabin until it was completely dark. Each and every muscle, bone, and joint pulled me back into Neverland. The next time I woke it was 4:00 a.m., dark, and Malcolm was still next to me, his breathing deep and even. Safety. Happiness. This is what I wanted. It would be so easy. Pack my stuff. Take off in his boat. But I couldn't leave my mom to the whims of Will and his family. Malcolm could walk away from his family and they'd still be safe. I had to somehow explain my failed mission and then I had to complete the second mission.

I reached up to touch his cheek and trace his lips. They were soft. I teased the ends of his hair and ran my fingers down the sides of his face to his neck. He grabbed my fingers and lifted them up to kiss one by one.

"I'm so glad you're okay," he said. "That I was there."

Was that a catch in his voice? An emotion? I pulled his head toward me. We kissed. Sweet. Innocent. But it only took a few seconds for it to deepen and turn passionate.

He broke off. "Run away with me. I have a plan in motion."

I bit my lip, desperate to say yes. "I can't."

He sighed. "I fear my family won't let me intervene in your next mission. They'll assume my feelings will cloud my judgment and I'll interfere."

"That's alright. I'll manage."

I rested my head against his chest. Tomorrow would be hard. We had to face his family. Would our deal be over because I failed to bring back pictures? Somehow I had to prove they still needed me. That I could do better. That I wouldn't betray them. Hopefully that would keep Mom, Dad and Constance safe and eventually this crazy nightmare would be over and we'd be a family again.

Malcolm's breathing deepened as he slept. I wanted to bottle this night and keep it with me forever. I wanted him to remember tonight, our whispered words, and the emotional ties. I slipped out from underneath his arm, my body still sore and aching, but I needed to return and report on my mission. I took one last look at him, sleeping peacefully.

The cool morning air brushed my skin and I breathed deep, ready to face the day and the challenges I'd face. At the end of the dock, I turned up the hill, dreading the talk I needed to have with Malcolm's family, without using him as a crutch or buffer.

I heard the boom first and then the sky burst into orange and red flames. Fiery arrows shot upwards and hungrily ate up the air. Pieces of wood flew, hitting the beach, the boats, and splashing into the sea. Black smoke billowed and blocked the early sun.

It was like the sea consumed his boat and then spit it out in pieces. I sprinted down to the dock. My cheek throbbed and every step sent pain shooting through my body. The smoke hit the back of my throat as I pushed through the thick vapors of dark gray.

"Malcolm!"

My throat closed up and I leaned over and gagged. Bits of the white hull floated in the water, left over debris. But it wasn't. It was a piece of my life. I searched for Malcolm, any sign of his head bobbing in the water. Any second he'd come to the surface with a smile and say, "Gotcha!"

But there was nothing. No sign of him. The dark waters pitched, laughing at me, unwilling to release its victim. I stared, begging it to let him go so I could save his life. Sirens sounded far away, but with every second, drew closer. Voices echoed from on the shore, curious onlookers wanting to know what had happened. I snapped my head up and peered into the dissipating smoke, wondering how this would look. Would I look guilty? How had I survived the explosion and not Malcolm? He reached from beyond the watery grave, urging me to run, to get to safety.

My heart bursting, I turned and sprinted. My feet slapped the dock, the sound sending me a message, reminding me of one fact.

I was alive. He wasn't.

Twenty-five

SMOKE STILL LINGERED IN my nostrils. The damp scent rose off my clothes and hair as I ran. I wanted. I needed to get lost. Let the coastal town wrap me up in her arms of vendors, white washed homes, and narrow streets. My chest heaved and tears blurred my vision.

Malcolm was dead.

Those three words repeated in my head. I ran harder. And longer. Ignoring the tourists I bumped, the kids I tripped over, and the head of lettuce rolling across the street. The vendors and their angry words yelled in Greek went right past me.

Malcolm was dead.

How could someone survive an explosion like that?

I kept running away from the answer even though it tugged on me, trying to yank me back to reality, back to the docks. Pain flashed through my side, screaming at me to stop. Pain felt good. After turning down street after street, my legs buckled and I fell, the pavement scratching my face and arms as I landed and rolled.

The sky filled with fluffy clouds spun above me, mocking me. I was aware of certain sounds: the sharp intake of each breath as my chest rose and fell, the pounding of my heart, and the pain jabbing through every part of me.

When an elderly man walked past and I heard his "tsk tsk," I pushed up and leaned against the wall of a nearby store. Streaks of dirt on the wall across the street blurred in and out of focus. Malcolm's family appeared one at a time in my mind: Edith, Bartholomew, Janelle, Will. I groaned. I had to tell them. Would their faces harden and they'd turn me away?

The walk back was long and slow, but eventually, I stood at their door. My hand paused in midair, trembling. The scrapes on my cheek and arms stung. My hand rested on the door and slowly dragged down. My fingers crossed over the grains in the wood.

"I'm sorry," I whispered.

The door opened and I fell into Will's arms.

"She's alive!" He pulled me into the house and shut the door.

The whole family surrounded me, smiling, talking, asking question after question. Janelle shouted something about food and I heard cupboards open in the kitchen.

Bartholomew immediately started arguing that I needed a stiff drink. They were taking care of me, concerned, assuming their son was okay. I hated to shatter it with the truth.

"Back away. Give her some room!" Will ordered.

He led me over to the couch and I sank into the cushiony softness. I scratched my finger over and over against the smooth fabric. I tried to talk, but every time I did, they shushed me. A cool washcloth pressed against my face. Someone dabbed at my arm. Janelle stroked my hand. Did this callused family, who mocked and joked about my death to my face, care about me? And had I learned to care for them despite it all? When you love someone that should extend to the ones they care about too. Shouldn't it?

While I debated this issue, I sensed Edith's stare. I couldn't look at her because everything that had happened was written on my soul, and she'd see right through me.

Will spoke. "When you didn't return, I went to the luncheon and I couldn't find you anywhere. Someone in the kitchen told me you'd left with a man."

Janelle placed a plate of fruit, cheese and bread on the coffee table. "That's when we figured Malcolm had rescued you from whatever trouble you got yourself into."

"Trouble?" I croaked. That was putting it mildly.

"Here, drink some more." Janelle offered me a glass.

I accepted it but couldn't bring it to my lips. No more stalling. The heartache increased, pressing, wanting release. My ears rang with the explosion and Malcolm's life going up in flames. "I have to tell you something..."

"Me first." Bartholomew coughed. "When Malcolm's boat exploded, we had no idea if you'd gone with him or not."

For the first time, I stared at all of them, one at a time. Maybe I'd misread this family. They seemed to love and care for each other deeply. Yet, they didn't seem bothered at all that Malcolm had died in an explosion. Had being assassins hardened them so much they couldn't mourn the loss of their son? Or had they truly kicked him out of their family and their hearts? My grief choked in my throat and my words spit out.

"I don't think I can do this." If that was what this life turned them into, I didn't want any part of it. I never wanted to stop caring about my family and the people I loved.

Edith spoke for the first time. "What kind of nonsense is that? We didn't spend weeks training you, for you to up and quit at the first sign of trouble."

"Trouble?" I asked, a simmering heat replacing the numb grief I'd felt since the explosion.

"The luncheon was her first real mission," Janelle argued in my defense. "It was probably too much."

The cane rapped on the floor. "Hogwash, I say."

They all spoke at once, arguing about whether I was ready or not for my upcoming mission. Their words flew like bullets, pinging off one another, the heat in the room rising. Their shallow words and lack of grief caused the simmering heat in me to turn into a full boil until I burst.

"What the hell is your problem?" I jumped to my feet and pointed at all of them. "How can you sit here and argue about whether I'm ready or not. Obviously I'm not. But that's not what matters here." I stopped, my breaths coming hard and fast.

They all turned their attention on me.

"Never mind that you put me in the way of a madman or that he stole the camera from me and I failed the mission. Thank God Malcolm knows enough of his own twisted family to understand I might be in trouble." My voice cracked but I pushed on. "But this isn't about me or the stupid camera. This is about Malcolm!"

At his name, the explosion returned all over again, the boom, the heat from the flames, the burning smoke. I dropped to my knees.

Janelle placed a soft hand on my shoulder. "You'll have to explain yourself. We're listening."

Edith snorted.

"I'm sorry." The strangled truth came out, my heart breaking with every word. "I couldn't save him. The debris.

The choppy water. It was impossible to see." I appealed to Janelle, the last of my strength dissolving and the tears that had threatened this whole time spilled down my cheeks. "I don't understand how you can all sit here and not care."

Janelle's mouth twitched. "It is such a shame."

"Yeah, we'll miss him dearly." Edith's snort turned in a cackle.

"I guess we'll have to call the funeral home!" Bartholomew could barely finish his sentence before he burst into a howl.

They all started laughing. Even Will smirked.

I backed away from them, ready to run for the door. "You guys are crazy."

My hand was on the knob when Will spoke. "I can't believe you fell for one of the oldest tricks in the book. Malcolm has been pulling that stunt since he could shoot a gun."

"What?"

Janelle led me back to the couch. "That's Malcolm's disappearing act. Trust me, the first time he pulled it we were all just as shocked. He rigged his tree house to blow when he was supposed to be spending the night in it. All because he was mad at us. I can't even remember what for now."

"That's right," Bartholomew said. "We took all his knives away from him for a whole month after scaring us like that."

"But there was no way he could've gotten off the boat that fast." Malcolm might've faked it before, but this was real. They had to see that.

"How long after you left the boat did it blow?" Edith asked.

"Well," I thought back, "I left the boat and walked up the dock."

Edith waved her hand. "Plenty of time for Malcolm to slip off the boat and onto a small dingy for this getaway. Trust me."

I slumped back onto the couch. It was an act? Malcolm had faked his own death? Without telling me? The realization sank in. He'd ask me to run away again. He said he had a plan in motion. I was the one who said no and slipped away after he'd rescued me. That must've told him I didn't care. That I was never going to run. I'd pushed him too far.

I was relieved he was alive and breathing, but the searing grief transformed into a numb disbelief.

As the next couple days passed, mainly in silence, my disbelief transformed into a quiet rage. When I obsessed about Malcolm ditching me and taking the easy way out, the dents in my bedroom wall and my aching hand suffered for it. I still had a ton of questions, but for the first time, the whole family avoided me. I tried to catch Edith alone by hanging out by the lemon bars, hoping she'd come out for a midnight snack, but she never did. Janelle would scurry away to scrub the upstairs toilet. Bartholomew would disappear into his office. And Will was rarely home.

I decided Edith was my best bet.

On the third night, out of frustration, I crept out to the kitchen and sat at the counter. The clock ticked and my temptation grew. My fingers twitched and tapped the granite. I traced the outside of the plate, itching to remove the plastic. I fiddled with the edge of the plastic wrap, slowly peeling it off, ready to drown my frustration in sugary goodness, even against my better judgment, and with the lingering memories that this family knew everything.

Whap!

Edith's cane, with the blade out, slapped against the counter, inches from my fingers. Her eyes were like cold balls of steel.

"I believe those are mine."

Twenty-six

I PRETENDED TO STRAIGHTEN the plastic wrap over the dish. "Just tightening. Wouldn't want them to go stale."

"Hmm." She pulled herself up onto the barstool. Her gaze drilled into me. "We don't quite trust you yet."

I didn't back down. "Then maybe I should leave because there's nothing more I can do."

She ran her fingers down the length of her cane and tapped the blade with her nails, trying to unnerve me. "Before we send you into the mission we brought you on board for, we need to know everything you know."

"But what if I don't know anything?" I glanced back to my bedroom and then at the front door.

"You could run. Go ahead." Edith nodded at the door. "But as soon as you step outside your life is free game, truce over."

Cold sweat prickled my neck.

She picked her cane off the counter and lay it on her lap, the blade still out. "You stole into the secret room and left prints all over a certain file. Betrayal just doesn't sit well with us."

I sighed. The past couple days, alone with my thoughts had worn me down, sucked the fight right out of me. "Fine. What do you want to know?"

"What do you know about Constance Gerald?" she asked.

"Seriously? Aren't we a little past that?" She rubbed her fingers over her cane again and I answered. "He's my mom's friend and he loves birds. Not much to tell." My voice shook. Technically it wasn't everything I knew but it was the truth.

Edith whacked the cane against the counter again. "No half-truths."

"I know he's a slime ball. He loves birds. I read in your files that he's recently come into a lot of money and that he had problems with Robert Yertsky." I stopped and racked my brain. Should I know more than that?

"Are you sure that's all?"

I decided to spit out the obvious. "You guys are planning to kill him. Robert hired you. My mom wants to protect him. I'm caught in the middle and praying to God my final mission isn't to assassinate him because I'm really not good when it comes to killing people."

"Hmm." She contemplated my answer while I sat on pins and needles. She shifted on the barstool. "What do you know about our families being life-time enemies?"

My confidence grew. The answer came immediately. "I learned in Paris that your family kills, I mean, takes care of important people heading into positions of powers where they might make bad decisions."

As the words left my mouth, they felt wrong. Constance Gerald was not a person of influence and not headed anywhere in life except maybe Argentina for a little bird watching. So why would he be on their hit list? Why were they taking paid jobs?

She huffed. "Continue."

"And my family believes in the sanctity of life and protects these people. You set up Jolie in Paris to draw my mom out and then set me up to see if I would follow in her footsteps. But the only reason I did was to find my mom and protect my friends."

"First," Edith said, "you deserve the truth so you can form opinions based on fact, not legend. Our "taking care" of certain individuals based on their position of power ended years ago. We were hired out by top government agencies in the 90s." She peeled back the plastic wrap and focused on the lemon bars. "But budget cuts left us in the cold. No real skills because we'd all been trained from birth for this career path. Janelle did a little accounting but it couldn't keep us afloat. So we've had to take personal jobs in the last few years or so, which we feel terrible about."

I sat with my spine rigid. A bit more prepared this time. "I understand you've all fooled yourself into thinking that taking a life is okay if they deserve it instead of going out and finding honest work."

"That's the answer I expected." Edith picked a lemon bar from the middle of the plate and took a bite. She chewed slowly, tormenting me. "One more question. What do you know about the monastery and the brethren of monks?"

I babbled for a bit, stalling, but the glint in her eye sharpened, so I answered. "That they're even more insane than all of you. They want to finish off both our families and we should probably work together and fight against them rather than fighting each other because this is about something bigger. I just have no clue what."

"You're right," she said. "It's about a lot more. Do you really want to know?"

I stood on the brink of knowledge, a breakthrough that would clear up any confusion. I couldn't fight back without knowledge and I couldn't rely on Malcolm's family or Adamos to protect my family forever. What if they weren't there?

"Yes, I want to know." My voice was strong and sure.

Edith took her time. She wiggled her fingers over the lemon bars again as if looking for the perfect one. They all looked perfect to me. Finally she chose one from the center and carefully rewrapped them. I wiped the drool from the corners of my mouth. She brought it to her mouth, then paused. I thought for sure she'd realized her grievous mistake and offer me one too.

"You know about our history. My family. Your family. But maybe you don't understand how far back our timeline runs." She sank her teeth into the bar, white powder dusting her lips.

"A couple hundred years?" I gazed longingly at the lemony goodness.

"Wrong." Except it sounded more like a muffled "wong". "Think farther, longer. Think bible times. Ancient Rome."

"Noah's ark?" I asked.

She huffed. "I'm not sure about that. But it goes back far enough that none of us know exactly when or how it started. Somewhere along the line, the secret information about our history disappeared."

I still didn't get it, and that must've been clear by the expression on my face.

"Meaning, that somewhere out there is a list. A family history."

"Like a scrapbook of your ancestry?" I asked.

"Almost. Except this information reveals everything. Names. Places. Dates. Targets. The government agencies involved. Behind-the-scene information that would rock the general public if it was to be revealed. Scandal would erupt. Basically, we'd be screwed and have to go into hiding or face prison time."

"Oh." Her words brought me back to the catacombs under Paris, to Adamos, before I knew his name, when he was still a prisoner. He'd been desperate to share information with me, his vision, of me.

"We believe the monks have the list."

"Why would they try to kill us over it?" I tried to keep my fingers from creeping closer to the plate. "And why are they after my family? We haven't killed anyone."

"Ha!" She pointed her crooked finger at me. "Not always, honey. You and your mom might be squeaky clean but I remember the stories my great grandmother told."

"What?"

"That's right." She hmpfed with satisfaction.

I took a few seconds to soak that in. Somewhere in the past, my family, my great, great grandparents were on the wrong side of the law? Or they worked for secret government agencies? Did Mom know any of this? It kinda made sense that the monks were trying to destroy us because of our line of work. But were they really trying to kill us? We were missing something, some clue, some aspect of this that would reveal everything.

Edith spoke. "Robert hired Constance to sneak into the monastery, find their secret room and steal scrolls. Constance received a lot of money upfront and didn't follow through with his responsibilities. At some point, his conscience caught up to him and he refused to continue."

"So Robert hired you guys," I said. "Seems like a lot for a bunch of old scrolls."

Edith shrugged. "There's probably more to it. But that's all I can tell you."

"Great, thanks." And in our moment of bonding, I reached for a lemon bar.

Edith gently slapped my hand. She pushed off the stool and grabbed her cane. Her tongue flicked out to catch the remaining powdered sugar on her lips.

"Oh, and by the way. Your last mission is tomorrow night."

Twenty-seven

EARLY THE NEXT MORNING, I whipped off my covers. My feet itched to feel the pavement and the morning run always helped clear my mind. Will had been in and out of the house and without Malcolm I'd been left to keep up with training.

After slipping into my clothes and my running sneakers, I walked straight past the lemon bars and outside into the crisp morning air. I breathed it in and stretched. Then I was off, finding my way through the dark, the slap of my sneakers echoing in the stillness. The roads twisted and turned and I found myself at the crest of a hill, sweaty and running on high.

I stretched my arms above my head. The marketplace lay before me like a blanket of twinkling jewels. Lights in the windows flickered and came on one by one as people woke for the day. Even farther lay the Mediterranean Sea and beyond that the monastery. And deep inside the stone walls, maybe locked away in a crypt or secret room was the list. All the information that threatened the lives of two families.

I took off running again, but as I got closer, my feet led me in another direction. The docks. Back to the sea and Malcolm. My legs felt like rubber but recovered quickly as I walked down the wooden slats and stopped where Malcolm's boat had been. The darkened sea was quiet this morning, whispering against the other boats and sliding onto the rocky shore.

I stared into the depths of the water, wishing for the answers to rise from its murky depths. I thought about our last time together, sleeping, cuddling, the whispered words, the kisses. My chest ached. I missed him, his touch, his smile, the sound of his voice, always reassuring, always encouraging. The water splashed against a boat with more force, the spray wetting my feet, as if telling me to leave this alone. Not to go there.

With or without Malcolm I had to do this last mission tonight for Malcolm's family. Prove to myself that I could protect my family. When this mission was done I'd confront Mom, tell her I was leaving to go find Dad and tell him the truth. And that she was welcome to come with me or stay.

The day passed quickly. Way too quickly. I stood in front of my dresser mirror, not recognizing the girl, the woman looking back at me. A green silk dress clung to every curve of my body with a line of jewels running across my collar bone and stretching up and over the shoulder strap. The material shimmered. Janelle's make-up job transformed me. Beautiful. Me?

I walked into the kitchen, the dress swishing around my legs, the heels clicking on the floor. Low whistles greeted me.

"You've outdone yourself, Janelle," Bartholomew said. "No wonder Malcolm fell for you, the foolish boy."

Edith nodded her approval, and Janelle hovered by the door with her hands clasped.

"No time to waste. The masque started an hour ago." Janelle motioned me forward.

"Where's Will?" I asked, tentative. Wouldn't he be the one to explain my mission?

Janelle smiled and winked.

"Right here." Will came down the stairs, strode over, and tucked his arm into mine.

I tried not to flush at how beautiful he looked. Chiseled. Like some Greek God visiting earth. But the grim smile told me he was all business. I wished I were standing next to his brother.

Janelle kissed my cheek then whispered in my ear. "Good luck, dear. We're rooting for you."

Edith rapped her cane. "Oh, stop with the mushiness, Janelle. That was always your weak point."

"Don't listen to her." Janelle patted my hand.

Then Will whisked me out the door to the waiting car with tinted windows. On the road, the wealthy neighborhood flashed by in a blur of lights and shadows. I clutched the matching green purse, my finger running over and over the silky material.

"You look way too nervous and guilty to pull this off. Relax," Will said. "You're going to burn a hole in your purse."

I dug my fingers into the purse and stayed calm. "Maybe I'd relax if you told me what I had to do."

"Do you really want to know? That might be worse."

I pried my clenched teeth apart. "Yes. I need to know."

Will cleared his throat and closed the window separating the driver and the backseat. He took hold of my hand and pulled me close as if we were lovers and he was whispering sweet nothings. His words tickled my ear and sent shivers racing down my back.

"You'll arrive alone at the masque. The woman of mystery. You will talk to no one but glide about the party from group to group as if you were mingling."

"But what about you?"

"We'll circle around and I'll arrive a few minutes after you. No one will know we're together but I'll be there, keeping an eye on you."

For some reason that didn't comfort me.

Will continued, "As soon as you can, find Constance. Follow him at a distance. At some point after he's had his fill of wine and women, he'll head out to the gardens for a cigar. He does this every party he throws."

What? "Whoa. You mean Constance is throwing this gig?" That meant Mom might be there. And Adamos. I didn't know if that was good or not. Probably not.

"After Constance leaves for the garden, you'll slip out of the main party room. Use the bathroom first just in case you're being watched. Find his study, his office. It won't be your typical office. You'll probably find lots of birdcages. They won't be making much noise because it's night and the shades on their cages will be pulled."

Yeah, I was familiar with the room.

He pulled me even closer, his lips brushing my skin. "In his desk, he keeps a flask of brandy. Open the flask and pour in the contents of the vial you will find in your purse. Stash it back in the same place and leave the party. The car will be waiting." He laughed as if we shared an intimate moment then pulled away.

"Wait a second," I yanked him back, "I said I wouldn't kill anyone!"

"Shh." He put a finger to his lips and glanced at the driver. "You're not. It's a drug. He'll fall asleep. I'll take care of the rest."

"You're going to kill him? Tonight? I can't be a part of that. You promised to stay away from him."

"Don't worry, I'm a man of my word. When I leave tonight, he'll still be alive. As you know, we like to know the whole story before taking action and there are still some missing pieces."

"Why do you need me?" I smoothed my hair as if that could smooth away my nerves too.

"If someone catches you wandering about, you can bat your eyes and claim to be lost. I can't get away with that. And he knows you. If anything goes wrong, he won't hurt you because of his relationship with your mother."

Oh, crap. "Will my mother be there?"

Will shrugged. "That we don't know. Be prepared for anything."

"What if she sees me?" She'd drag me out like a two year old.

Will placed a gift on my lap. A mask made of green silk. Diamonds bejeweled the outlines of the eyes and green and red feathers plumed out from the top and the sides. I ran my fingers over the tiny studded nubs.

"Feel better?" Will asked.

"Not really."

We rode the rest of the way in silence. The growing pit of terror in my stomach made me want to stop the car and puke. Too many things could go wrong with this night. Right before the car stopped, Will leaned over. He fitted the mask over my eyes and dug small combs into the back of my hair to keep the mask in place.

He traced a finger down my arm and kissed my cheek. "You look stunning by the way. Go get 'em, killer."

I stepped out of the car. Alone. He was so not funny.

Twenty-eight

THE CAR PULLED AWAY, and I stood frozen at the start of the path leading to the front door. Music spilled from the window and lanterns swung in the breeze. Every flowering bush seemed to be in perfect bloom and the lawn meticulously landscaped, just like I remembered. Except, last time, I was an uninvited guest and failed my mission.

Another car pulled up to the curb, so I scooted up the path, my hands clutching my purse like it was a life preserver. I couldn't keep my mind off the vial with the sleeping drug. It pulsed through the silk against my fingers reminding that I was an almost assassin. And I didn't like it.

The man at the door checked my forged invitation and waved me in. I'd decided to play up the mysterious woman in green and not say a word. I followed the hallway and entered the party room, trying to not trip on my heels.

I drifted from group to group, playing up the charade that I knew people but not talking to anyone. The women were all beautiful, dressed in many different colors, with jewels dripping from their necks and fingers and elaborate masks hiding their faces. The men all wore black and white tuxedos, most of them older and showing it with their paunchy stomachs. I searched for Constance and my mom. I assumed she'd be here and on the alert for any action that Will's family might make. She wouldn't be looking for me and I was sure that was the plan.

The small orchestra in the corner played everything from classical music to the Beatles. The room swayed as couples circled the dance floor. Even I swayed back and forth as I stood by the buffet table, taking it all in. The appetizers and dishes smelled delicious but the thought of eating turned my stomach.

I felt the gentle touch around my waist first and soft Greek words in my ear second. I jumped and pulled away. Adamos offered his hand.

Then he spoke in English, "Would the beautiful lady like to dance?"

"Why yes, she would." My heart leapt for joy as I followed him onto the dance floor.

A new song started and he whisked me across the floor, the room blurring. I tried my best to remember the dancing lessons, but it was all I could do to stay on my feet. We finally got into rhythm and I waited. And then I waited and waited. I assumed he'd tell me to do something just like everyone else.

Do that. Do this. Not what do you think about this? What are you comfortable with? Nope. It was do this or possibly die. Not many options. When the colors of the party blurred together, my mind wandered.

What if this was Malcolm dancing with me, his arms around me, his voice whispering in my ear. We'd dance the whole night away and let any worries or pressures from our family drop off piece by piece. The room would fade and it would be just him and me. Then we'd go back to his boat for a private party afterward.

"You seem sad," Adamos said.

I smiled and pushed Malcolm out of my mind. The song slowed and he showed no intentions of letting me go, but twirled me under his arm just in time for me to see Constance enter the room with Mom on his arm. I sucked in my breath. She was stunning. I'd never seen her so dolled up. Her mask sprouted a rainbow of feathers that framed her face.

"Is something wrong?"

I shook my head.

He followed my gaze to Constance and my mom. "A couple years ago, a woman washed up on the shores of our monastery, barely alive, barely breathing. I found her and nursed her back to health." He hesitated, then said, "That woman was your mother."

I bit down on my lip. What?

He continued. "I felt it was my calling to protect her. Then the visions from God started. The brethren couldn't argue with that. We all have our calling in life. Just like you struggle to put your family back together."

My throat tightened.

"The monks may live in the shelter of stone walls, but they're not ignorant of the evil in this world. They followed me just as a mother might follow her child. They discovered the connection between your mother and a family of assassins they'd been seeking for decades. Over the years, both sides have murdered in the name of God. And they felt called to bring swift justice for the slain."

He twirled me in his arms and circled me round the dance floor again. "It is my duty to protect you after leading my brethren to you." He ducked his head as if ashamed. "I'm here. Go do what you have to do."

The song ended and Adamos led me to the edge of the dance floor, then melted into the landscape like he does so well. I drifted through the clumps of party guests twittering like canaries and giggling from champagne while the truth replayed in my head. Mom had crashed on the shores of the monastery barely alive? What had happened?

Before I could do anything, someone brushed against me and briefly grasped my hand. I turned to see the back of my mom's blue velvet gown swishing behind her.

In my hand was a note. It said, "Meet me in the bathroom."

Twenty-nine

I PUSHED OPEN THE bathroom door and realized this could go really, really bad. Mom would be absolutely pissed that I showed up here, working for the other team.

As soon as the door clicked shut, Mom smiled. She flushed the toilet, then put a finger to her lips and motioned for me to lock the door. She turned on the faucet and let the water run as if someone was washing their hands. I wanted to say, "Mom, really? I doubt anyone bugged the bathroom." But if I spoke she'd probably kill me. I wouldn't have to wait for the monks.

Then she turned total spy on me. She pulled out a small black box with a tiny switch from her drawstring purse and flicked it on.

"Okay, we can talk but not for long." She focused her full attention on me, her eyes devoid of compassion and understanding. "I was absolutely appalled when I heard from Mr. Rottingham you never arrived. But we'll talk about that at another time."

"What is that thing?"

"It's a scrambler. If there are bugging devices nearby then whoever is listening on the other end will get nothing but static."

I huffed. "We're in the bathroom."

"That's a beautiful dress, Savvy. Who bought it for you?"

Was this a trick question? I hesitated but then said, "Will's family."

"That was nice of them." She ran her fingers along the collar of the dress and touched the embedded diamonds. "I suppose you're working for them tonight."

I nodded. "Mom, it's okay. Constance isn't in trouble tonight."

She glanced sharply at me, then grabbed my hand. "Feel along your dress, along the diamonds."

I did.

"Do you feel the thin wire between the stones and inside the seam?"

I wanted to scoff but pressed my fingers against the material, hoping and wanting to find nothing. But there it was. A thin piece of what felt like wire in the seam. My face must have shown my disbelief because Mom nodded with satisfaction.

"They've heard everything you've said so far tonight and everything you will say."

It seemed obvious to me. "They want to protect me, Mom. Make sure I'm okay."

She slapped the side of my cheek with a sharp clap. Tears stung my eyes but I left my hands by my sides.

"What will it take for you to get it? They're not your friends. Sure they act nice, like they're training you, helping you. Just in exchange for a few favors."

My stomach felt queasy at her words.

"I've been there. Right where you are. Sucked into Will's world, influenced by his promises. All up until the point where Will tried to kill me when they didn't need me. Don't you understand? You're playing with fire. One you can't put out when the game is done."

I remember what Adamos told me about Mom arriving on the shores of the monastery barely alive. I gulped. That must've been on one of her weekends away. A scrapbooking trip.

"Why did you let him influence you? Why did you do it?" I asked, wanting to understand. Then maybe I'd understand my decisions too.

"That's not a story for right now."

"What I have with Will's family is different. They wouldn't hurt me. We have a deal."

She shook her head. "When are you going to wake up? That deal will only last until you give them what they want.

Then you will be expendable. One more loose thread they can't afford."

I backed away. No. They wouldn't do that. Would they?

Mom glanced at the scrambler. "We only have a couple more minutes before they figure out what's going on. What are you supposed to do for them tonight and tell me the truth."

My voice trembled. "I'm causing a little distraction so Constance will be unavailable for a bit."

She narrowed her eyes. "What kind of distraction?"

I squirmed.

"Tell me. Hurry."

"I'm supposed to slip a sleeping drug into the flask of brandy in his desk so he'll sleep. Will didn't really tell me what was going to happen next, but I'm pretty sure Constance will be okay for tonight because they're pretty thorough with making sure people are guilty first." I stopped talking because I ran out of breath.

Mom bit back a laugh. "Oh my God, Savvy. They're assassins. Have you forgotten that?"

My back prickled in defense. "I'm not stupid."

Mom's face softened. "I know that. You're smart. Too smart to have gotten mixed up with them."

I wanted to tell her that I was doing this for her and Dad, so they'd be safe and so that when this big mess was over we could be together again, happy, safe, and a family once more. But what if she didn't want that anymore?

"Our time is up. You have to trust me. I'll take the vial. I'll do the drugging. Will is not a passive killer. He would never kill with poison. Too easy and not enough of a challenge for him. When Constance falls asleep, I'll hide in the shadows, and wait and see what Will does. If he goes to hurt Constance, I'll do whatever I can to protect him."

Her words rushed over me, sparking a panic that spread to my limbs. This was becoming way too real. Mom talked like she knew Will, really knew him. But she didn't fully understand my side of the story.

"Mom, you've got to listen to me."

She cut me off. "I have to turn this off or they'll get suspicious. His whole family is probably listening. I'll do the work. Leave the party now. Adamos is here. He'll take you home. When I get back, we'll call Dad and make plans to meet in England. How about that?"

Then Mom turned off the scrambler making it impossible for me to explain. She gave me a quick hug and kissed the side of my cheek. She pulled the vial out of my purse, without giving me much of a choice, and then she left.

I slumped onto the toilet lid and pulled my legs up to my chest. She didn't let me finish, but that was probably her plan. She didn't want to hear my arguments or hear me defend

Will or his family. If this wasn't about my family, I'd gladly go with Adamos, but Mom didn't know the whole truth. I pressed my forehead to my knees, confused. As much as I wanted to trust Mom and go obediently outside and leave with Adamos, I needed to finish this mission for my family and Constance. I'd promised. But what if Mom was serious about leaving to get Dad? And that was the problem.

Were any of them telling the truth?

Thirty

ANYTHING COULD HAPPEN TONIGHT. But I knew one thing for sure. I couldn't sit in the bathroom forever.

I dug around in my purse thankful for Edith's training session on cool spy gadgets. Dad would be in spy heaven. I found the lipstick tube that was a nice shade of red. I turned the doorknob and then shut the door so there was no click. I'd kicked off my high heels so my feet were a whisper on the floor. Because of the catastrophe with the vase, I knew exactly where to find the office filled with the birds. I opened the door a crack, but Mom wasn't there. I had to find her before she drugged the flask.

I returned to the ballroom and let the flamboyant music lead me in the right direction. The party swirled with colors and noise. The laughter was louder. The voices more belligerent as the wine flowed freely.

A flash of my Mom's velvet dress left the room in the direction of the gardens. It dawned on me that Mom might've lied to me. Maybe she was on her way to Constance. I cut straight through the dancing couples much to their annoyance. I didn't bother with excuse me, not if Will was listening to my every word.

At the edge of the room by the open door, I peered into the gardens. The sweet aroma of flowering plants gave me a false sense of security. The large ferns and low hanging flowers offered perfect hiding places and I moved from one umbrella to another until I smelled smoke. Cigar smoke. And I heard Mom's voice.

"Constance, please, we need to talk."

"Marisa dear, it's a party. We can talk later."

I cringed at his frivolous tone of voice that told me he had no clue what was going on behind his back.

"There are things we must talk about." Mom insisted. "Tonight."

Constance took his time answering, probably trying to figure out some kind of concocted story to get Mom off his ass. "How do I put this?" Smoke puffed into the air above their heads. "This is a party."

Mom persisted. "Please, listen to what I have to say."

Prickles ran down my arms. Mom sounded bitter. Again, I felt the power of her past with Will and his family. If only she trusted me to tell me everything. Then again, I wasn't telling her everything either.

"Marisa, Marisa. Let's talk about more pleasant subjects like the next bird watching expedition we must take together. Damn," Constance muttered. "My cigar went out and my light's inside. If you'd excuse me, I'll be right back."

"No problem. Let me hold your drink for you?"

"Thanks, darling."

Constance left and I panicked. Mom would pour the vial in now but it needed to happen in the office. If Constance fell asleep in the gardens then guests or servants could stumble upon him, and I wouldn't be following the plan. I couldn't wait. The swiftness and obvious skill of my movements surprised me. Somewhere along the line I'd truly become the secret agent. With lipstick in hand, I approached Mom without a sound, twisted up the needle and stabbed her neck. Guilt flooded my veins as the drug flooded hers.

She turned and disbelief flashed across her face, then sadness. "Savvy?"

"Sorry, Mom," I whispered it over and over.

She slumped over, the drug taking effect, and I dragged her behind the bench and landscaping. Thankfully the bushes weren't pruned too short. I laid her down gently on a pile of mulch and moved the hanging leaves to hide her body. It didn't take long to find the vial tucked down the front of her dress.

Her eyes fluttered. "Savvy." Her one word spoke volumes. She wanted to know why.

I whispered to her again. "Please forgive me. I'm just trying to protect you and get our family back together again."

"Oh, Savvy." Then her head lolled to the side and her eyes closed.

I'd be back.

I practically ran to his office. Various birdcages with shades pulled on them filled the room. I went straight to the desk, opening and shutting drawers until I found his flask in the left bottom one. The cap unscrewed easily and I poured the contents of the vial into it and then sloshed it around. Cap back on, I placed it carefully back in the drawer.

Footsteps sounded in the hall. I rushed to the far corner of the room and crouched behind a rather large floor cage.

The door flew open and Constance rushed into the room. "I've got you!"

Thirty-one

I EXPECTED THE LIGHTS to flick on and the alarm bells to ring with the announcement that there was an intruder in his inner sanctum. But the lights never came on. His feet slapped against the floor, and he headed in my direction like he knew where I was hiding.

His large shadowy form appeared first and then his face. "Why good evening, Savvy. How nice of you to drop by."

He wore goggles. Night vision goggles. Like he'd invaded my mom's secret stash of spy gadgets. Or she'd given him access because I'd looked and never found it.

"I said good evening, Savvy." He pushed the goggles back on his head, causing his hair to stick up in all directions.

"Um, hello. Nice cage collection." I scrambled to my feet.

He held out his hand. I took it with my teeth clenched.

"You really should've mentioned you were crashing the party, I would've sent you an invitation." He strutted over to his desk and then whipped around. "Your mother would've loved to see you."

His pointed words caused a burn to rise from my neck to the roots of my hair. He set a chair near his desk that had been standing against the wall.

"Please, sit."

I glanced at the door as if maybe I could make a run for it but Will's words were branded in my brain, so I took a seat. I had to make sure Constance drank his liquor and fell into dreamland. And then get Mom to safety.

"I'd love to show off some of my darlings but they're all asleep. You'll have to visit sometime with your mother." He put a finger to his lips. "But wait, you're not living with her, are you?"

I forced a laugh. "Not at the moment. I moved in with friends."

"Hmm. Interesting."

I rubbed the silk fabric of my dress between my fingers as he drummed his against the desk.

"So how about those magpies?" I asked.

He gave me a funny look. "I know you don't care about my birds."

"True. But you're friends with my mom and she's shown a sudden interest in birds."

"Let's not pretend."

Pretend? "Sure, let's not."

"Would you like a night cap?" he asked, opening his desk drawer.

"I'm not allowed to drink. You know my mom." I rolled my eyes as if I were some rebellious teenager.

He poured a bit from his flask into a cup and pushed it toward the edge of the desk.

"I'm sure she won't mind. We're on the same team." He downed a shot and let out a sigh. The grip he had on the flask relaxed.

I pressed the cup to my lips and pretended to drink. He poured himself another one. His words struck a chord deep inside. On the same team? I wanted to be a team player but Mom wouldn't let me. That was why I ended up at Malcolm's house. But tonight? Directly disobeying Mom, and letting the man she was trying to protect get drugged? What if she was right about Will?

He poured another shot.

Did I want his life on my conscience? He went to down it and I grabbed it from him and threw it to the ground.

He spluttered. "Are you mad?"

Then he smacked his lips as if tasting the liquor for the first time. He sniffed the open flask and then absently ran his hand down his pant leg. I could see the clues lining up in his mind, spelling out my guilt as if we were playing a family Scrabble game.

I gulped and inched toward the edge of my seat, ready to run.

He gripped the flask, his knuckles turning white and his face various shades of red. When he spoke his words came out stilted. "What's going on here?"

I shrugged. "I'll go check with Mom." And I started to walk away.

His hand snaked out and grabbed onto my wrist. He yanked me close, his alcohol breath beaming down on me. "Don't play games with me, girl."

"I'm sure I can find her. Teamwork, right?" I squeaked. "I think I hear her calling me." I tried to pull away but his grip was like iron.

He shook his head as if trying to clear away cobwebs. Was the drug already working?

"I don't hear a thing and I think it's time you get a taste of your own medicine." He reached up into my hair and yanked my head back. "I'm not stupid. I know what you and your mom are doing."

He pushed the tip of the flask to my lips and tipped it. The liquor gushed, spilling down the sides of my face. The little that made it into my mouth left a burning trail down my throat and into my chest. I struggled but I couldn't move an inch.

He pulled it away and let me breathe. I gasped for air and wiped my mouth. Then he yanked my head back again and forced me to drink. I coughed, spitting it back up but he wouldn't stop. When the flask was empty, he threw it across the room and pushed me into the chair.

"I know your Mom doesn't love birds. I knew back at the National Gardens." He leaned forward so his face was inches from mine. "A true bird lover would care more about the birds and their well-being than themselves. Oh yes, I've known for a while. Just waiting. And now I know. You were working for her all along. You're both out to get me."

"No, that's not the way it is." Mom thought she'd had him fooled this whole time.

He leaned back in his chair. "Then please, enlighten me, dear Savvy."

I blinked, the room spinning a bit.

"I know. Terrible when someone drugs you, isn't it?" Constance remarked.

I gripped the chair, wanting to run but knowing I wouldn't make it very far. How soon would Will arrive? "You want the truth?"

Constance's eyes brightened. "That would be nice."

"There's a family of assassins trying to kill you."

He burst out laughing. "Right. And your mom is my guardian angel sent from heaven?"

"Well, yeah, kinda. My family is at odds with the group of assassins and we try and protect their targets, which is why my mom went out of her way for you."

"Tell me another one."

His face blurred and I felt the incredible need to sleep. "I'm serious. You need to pack your stuff and run far away from here."

He leaned closer. "And who would want to kill me?"

I felt like I knew the answer but the words were just out of grasp. And then Robert's face flashed through my mind. "Oh, I don't know, perhaps your partner you pissed off?"

A voice echoed down the hallway. "Constance!"

His face paled and he placed his hands on either side of my face. "Dear girl, you're telling the truth, aren't you?"

"Yes," I managed to say even though he was squeezing my cheeks together.

Footsteps sounded in the hall, nearing the office. The color drained from his face, and sweat beaded on his forehead.

"Holy blue-footed boobie," he muttered.

"I'm sorry. My mom's been working to protect you, not hurt you."

"Yes, yes, I see that now." He grabbed my arm, pulled me across his body and shoved me under his desk. "Stay there," he hissed. "Don't make a sound."

"Constance!"

I shuddered in response to the familiar voice and flashed back to an earlier mission.

Thirty-two

THE COLD METAL OF the desk was clammy against my cheek. The words between Constance and me pricked my conscience. I'd warned him. And he didn't believe me. Angry voices pounded against my skull, unrelenting. Their sharp staccato tones were like nails being hammered through my head.

"You were my partner, damn it!"

That voice again. Robert Yertsky. He was obviously tired of waiting for the hired assassins to do their job. I pushed up and leaned to the left so I wouldn't miss anything.

"I know, I'm sorry. I lost it or someone must've stolen it," Constance said, his words slurring a bit from the drugged brandy.

"Lost it? You're the one who's lost it if you think I'm going to believe some fan dangled story about losing the map! We both agreed to wait it out and then go back for scrolls."

Constance slammed his fist against the desk. The vibrations rippled through the metal and against my back.

"You were the one who wanted the map. You didn't want to return the scrolls, but my conscience couldn't bear it anymore." His voice dropped low as if he were a child admitting his guilt. "I still refuse to participate in this. It's wrong."

"What?" Robert asked in a strangled voice.

"You whispered words in my ear about lost treasure and riches and how easy it would be. I have enough money now and want out. You can keep everything!" Constance stood and moved away from the desk. "Greed. That's what this is about. I never should've listened to you."

"Oh no, dear friend. You're wrong. You have enough money because I paid you a tidy sum."

Constance's voice caught. "What do you mean by that?"

"Betrayal. It never leads to anything good."

"What are you talking about? Betrayal?" Constance huffed. "I've done nothing but keep our secret and our friendship. I just want out."

Anger escalated and their words became increasingly harsh and mean. I could've used a partner, but I'd drugged the only person who could help. It was up to me.

"Our friendship, our partnership could've been so much more, dear friend." Robert sighed. "I wished things had turned out differently. Unfortunately, someone stole the copy of the map you gave me and I want yours."

I cringed, shrinking into myself a little bit more.

Constance huffed. "I told you. I lost it."

"I don't believe you," Robert stated.

I wanted to pinch Constance or send him a text and tell him to get the hell out of here and away from Robert. His partner was a loose cannon. Constance, who once repulsed me, suddenly had my compassion. He seemed clueless to the real danger of his situation. A little like me.

Robert continued, "I didn't want to be the one to do this. But you know the saying. If you want something done right then do it yourself."

"What's that supposed to mean?" A hint of fear lay under Constance's question.

I huddled under the desk and wrapped my arms around my legs. Frantically, I tucked any evidence of my dress under my body. Robert would strangle me on the spot if he knew.

"Quite simple. You aren't needed anymore. I never should've brought you on board."

The cocking of a gun rattled through the room.

"Robert! No!" Constance cried.

"Tell me where you hid your copy of the map! I need to find that secret room! More scrolls! More money!" A warning bullet pinged, and a window shattered. "Traitor!"

"How am I a traitor?" Constance shifted his stance as if ready to flee. "You had the map."

"Liar!" Robert yelled, his voice bordering on madness.

My whole body shook. Constance could reveal me as the thief, put my life in danger and protect his own. But he wasn't. He was protecting me. Every evil thought I had about this man I took back. I pressed my forehead against my knees, self-deprecating thoughts beating me down.

"I could let the professionals take care of you," Robert threatened, "but I'm going to find this rather gratifying."

"Professionals?" Constance asked, not able to hide the quiver in his voice.

"That's right. But they're moving a little too slow for me. You'd think assassins would take care of the job. But no, they want to make sure you're truly guilty."

That would be Will's family. At least they were assassins with morals, but somehow that didn't make me feel any better. Just six months ago I was the target of their slow scrutiny.

"Hand over the map, and I'll spare your life. We'll go our separate ways," Robert warned, his voice rising in pitch.

"Fine." A drawer slammed open, papers rustled about, then it slammed shut. "Take it," Constance spit out.

The gunshot rang loud and clear and Constance slumped to the ground next to me. I froze, my heart thudding. The roar and ringing in my head blocked out everything else. Murder. A body. About five inches from me.

"Thank you. But sorry, dear friend. You are no longer trustworthy." The door slammed behind him.

I was shaking, replaying the words in my head and seeing Constance fall to the ground. I peeked and he was still there. But wait! His chest was moving, up and down, ever so slightly. I scrambled out and grabbed his hand. He groaned.

"It's okay. You're going to make it." I didn't care that Will and his family could hear everything through the wire in my dress. Will would probably be here any second but I had to go. I couldn't face him.

"Come here," Constance groaned, the words slipping out at the same time.

I stroked his hand. "Shh. Help is on the way."

"Come close. I have a secret."

"Wait." I grabbed hold of the jewels on my dress and with a yank ripped them off and revealed the wire. With a tug, I pulled it out and threw it across the room, then I leaned over. "What, Constance?"

"False map. I burned real one."

"Huh?"

He gripped my hand with a surge of strength. "Someone needs to know."

217

And then in short bursts, he revealed the details of the map, the route to the secret room in the monastery where he believed I'd find more scrolls. He'd memorized the map and burned the real one. As he spoke these last words, his head rolled to the side and he passed out. I lay my hand on his chest and breathed in relief at the faint heartbeat pulsing against my fingers.

I said goodbye. I made my apologies with tears dropping onto his chest. Then I fled from the man I'd judged wrong, from my own cowardice, and from my bad decisions.

Thirty-three

I RUSHED OUT OF the study but stopped in the hallway and not just because my legs were still wobbly. I leaned against the wall to control my breathing. Robert would be long gone. Eventually someone would call the police and they couldn't find me or question me as eyewitness to the scene. This all had to be kept under wraps.

I wanted Malcolm. I wanted him to hold me and tell me that we had a happy ending. I needed to be close to someone who understood this whole mess and didn't want to be part of it either. There was only one place I wanted to go. The docks. I needed to hear the quiet lap of the water and smell the sea air. Everything that reminded me of him.

Sounds from the party drifted down the hall. A dark shadow approached. I pressed against the wall. Adamos stepped out of the darkness and nodded, motioning to me. Was he mad at me?

"Adamos?" My voice came out hoarse.

He turned with a finger on his lips and shook his head.

"I ripped out the wire. Constance is barely alive and Mom..." The words died before I could say what I did out loud.

Tears burned and his face softened. He closed the gap between us quickly and wrapped me in a hug.

He whispered in my ear. "I believe in you. Do what you have to do."

"Mom?"

"I found her, but she's still out of it. I'll take care of her." He kissed my cheek in a big brother kind of way then rushed to take care of Constance.

The rocky shore called to me, the gentle waves whispering with the tide without a care, the cool breeze, the salt air. I stumbled down the hall, not anything like a graceful spy maneuvering in and out from her mission. So many thoughts tumbled around in my head, needing to be heard, demanding freedom and recognition. I tried my hardest to float through the small pockets of partiers, pretending to know them, but I think I looked more like the spurned lover running from a scene. Or the guilty criminal.

The cool air outside brushed my face and lifted my spirits. With my dress in my hand so I wouldn't trip, I started the long walk to the docks. I stumbled and then looked back to see what I'd tripped over. A pale meaty arm lay across the path.

A sick feeling formed in my stomach. An arm stretched out on the ground from the landscaping was not a good sign. I recognized the shirt. My heart sank. On tiptoes, I moved to the other side of the bush to find the rest of the body. A knife jutted out from his chest with dark blood streaming, soaking his shirt and pooling on the ground.

Robert.

I cringed, fighting the desire to just run. But what if he still had the map? With one eye closed and one eye open I patted his shirt. I almost puked when searching his pockets and when I had to lift his body to look underneath. Nothing. The map was gone. Poor guy didn't have a chance. The question was who?

Laughter came down the gravel path. Guests leaving. They'd discover the body for sure. I fled, and for the first time, I thanked Will for those early morning runs. Of course, running in a gown was not quite as easy.

I reached the docks just as the moon peeked out from the clouds and cast its silvery beams across the water. Any other night this would be romantic. The spot where Malcolm's boat would've been moored was a gaping hole. An ache pushed up from my chest. I dug my feet into the sand and walked down the beach to a small rocky overhang. The shadows would hopefully keep me hidden.

"Sorry, Malcolm," I whispered into the night.

I huddled against the rock. If he were here he'd understand I felt sick to my stomach at the sight of the dead body, the blood, the paling face of the victim. Maybe he'd seen enough dead bodies and that was why he was willing to walk away. Maybe he'd learned the hard truth that life would go on with or without him.

I tried to cry, but the tears wouldn't come. I wanted to scream. The timing was perfect. I was by myself. No one was looking for me. The darkness hid me from my own humiliation but all I could do was stare numbly out at the water. The cooler ocean breeze sent prickles along my bare arms but I didn't care. All I could see were dead bodies lining up, falling in a pile, their vacant eyes, staring.

Robert's body and blood stained my mind. I held my hands up in front of me, imaginary blood coating my skin and dripping down my arm and into the sand. I took part in his death. My stomach roiled and I couldn't stop the feeling of nausea that rushed up into my throat. I turned and lost it in the sand. After taking a few minutes to get control, I turned and wiped my mouth.

I wasn't sure how much time passed—maybe an hour—but a cloud cut off the moon and darkened the sky. I had to make this right. I had to go home and force Mom to talk with me or at least listen as I told her my truth in all this. I wanted my family back. I pushed off the sandy ground, my legs stiff from being tucked underneath, and my head throbbing.

I stood outside the door, wavering on what to do. I put my hand on the knob, then pulled it away, then raised it to knock, then let it drop to my side. Do I knock? Would they want me to just enter? I opened it a crack and peered in. Completely dark. They weren't back yet. I stumbled through, my legs not wanting to support me anymore. I felt like a stranger as I walked through the kitchen. I couldn't be here, not without them. I grabbed the blanket from the couch and made my way outside. Wrapped in a blanket and sitting on a lawn chair, I stared into the shadows.

The blank eyes of dead people stared at me everywhere I looked. The darkness draping the lawn and covering the trees became blood. Every jagged branch that pierced the air became a knife.

Robert was dead.

Robert was dead.

It could've been me. Or Mom. Or Constance. I'd never know. Mom's words about Will hovered in the air, whispering their warning. "Trained assassin. He's nice at first. He can change in the blink of an eye." Did Will have me fooled? Maybe his whole family did. I shook my head. I didn't believe that.

The door creaked behind me. I held my breath and clutched the blanket like it could protect me from the hard truth. Even if I didn't want to go back, I had to.

"Savvy?" Adamos's voice was deep and rich, like chocolate cake that matched the color of his eyes.

"Will Constance make it?" I asked.

"He has a long recovery but he'll make it. Your mother would like to talk to you."

"Is she okay?" I croaked.

He stood in front of me, blocking my view of the knife-like branches, for which I was grateful.

"Yes." He was silent for a moment and I knew the reprimand was coming. "But your actions tonight put your mother in a lot of danger. She was left defenseless with her mortal enemy nearby."

"You mean Will?"

"Yes, he means Will." Mom stood by Adamos. I hadn't even heard her cross the lawn.

Thirty-four

ADAMOS NODDED AND LEFT. Like somehow he wanted me to know he didn't approve so I'd apologize.

"May I sit with you?" Mom asked.

"It's your house." Sarcasm. Not my best trait but it sprang up like a shield before I could stop it.

"It's your house too."

"Is it really?" I asked.

"You are welcome here. Always. No matter what."

I swallowed my ego, ashamed of my desperation and misguided attempts at protecting her that night. "Even though I could've gotten you killed?"

Mom nodded and silence wedged between us making it seem like I was back in France when she felt so far away. I sucked it up.

"I'm sorry. It was stupid what I did but Will would not have hurt you."

Mom's head whipped up and her eyes jabbed at me, sudden tension emanating from her body. "Don't for one second think you have that man figured out. Don't think because he was nice to you one day that he will be the next day and don't think that because he tells you he's there to protect you that he actually means it."

Tears burned my eyes. Will and his family trained me, made me stronger, but they were never my family. "They wouldn't hurt me. We made a deal."

Mom talked louder. "They don't make deals. They make false promises when it suits them."

Frustration pounded at my insides. "Just because he betrayed you doesn't mean he'll do it to me."

"Betray me?" Her voice cracked. "He tried to kill me. I had to go into hiding which meant I could never see you, never talk to you, never hear your voice or laughter or hold you in my arms." Her words rushed out, pooling at my feet and trying to suck me in. "You want to know the truth? Really know the truth?"

"Yes."

"Once he thought I was dead, I couldn't go back to you and Dad. They were watching you both, waiting, testing to see if I had really died." She reached over and grabbed my hand. "I stayed away from my family, from my husband and you, hoping, praying that he'd leave you alone."

I whipped my hand away. "Don't you think I know that? Malcolm told me everything in Paris. They'd laid the trap for you and then I got sucked in and they found out you're alive because of me."

Truth hit me square in the chest and the realization poured out that I felt guilty for stumbling into the truth and putting my mom in danger.

"If I hadn't tried so damn hard to find you, you'd still be safe and I'd still be living with Dad, miserable. But I don't care because I got you back and I hate that I risked it all for nothing, because you don't include me."

By the time the last word left my mouth, my heart had cracked and the deep hidden hurt places, the dark truths we carry around but can't see and don't want anyone else to see leaked out. Exposed. Everything I wanted her to know but feared she'd see.

"Oh, Savvy. But you were with your dad!"

"What?" Bitterness dripped from my mouth, leaking out the sides and coating my words like poison. "After you left it wasn't the same. He withdrew. And then he got all involved with Spy Games and the only thing he talked to me about was spy stuff, which is kind of ironic. And then you dragged me here without letting me say goodbye or explain."

She slumped over. "I'm sorry. There's no excuse for any of this. All I wanted to do was protect you and your father. I sensed you both were struggling, but I couldn't reveal myself."

Her words echoed my thoughts. The whole time I'd been with Will and his family that was my justification. Protect my family. But looking at Mom hunched over told me that maybe I'd hurt her too. Maybe I'd made the wrong decision.

"Why did they invite you into their home?" Her voice was soft and made me want to sit next to her and put my head on her shoulder so she could stroke my hair and rub my back like she did when I was a kid.

"He offered to train me in exchange for your safety. But I think they wanted me for tonight, for my connection to Constance, so I could sneak in."

"Honey. They could do any of that by themselves. You know the phrase, keep your friends close?"

I knew it. They'd never needed me. They wanted to keep an eye on me while entrancing me in their spell. And they used me to get to Malcolm, to bring him home again.

"Alright. My girls need some refreshments."

Adamos bustled out and put a tray on the rickety table. He placed a candle next to it and lit it with a match. A small flame burst toward the sky and fell back to a whisper, flickering in the breeze. But the warm light couldn't fix the raw emotions Mom and I had dished out.

Adamos fixed us both a plate of crackers and cheese. "You both need to eat and we need to plan."

"What?" We both said at the same time.

"Sorry, but I could not help but overhear a part of your conversation and it seems that for too long you both have been the ones running, the ones scrambling to understand why your lives were falling in pieces around you, why someone was trying to kill you and why your family was ripped apart. Time to protect yourselves."

He settled into the third chair, letting his words soak in. I glanced at Mom then quickly looked away as her eyes met mine. Was it possible? That she and I could work together?

"What can we do?" I asked feebly then nibbled on a cracker. My nerves stretched thin as if I knew the answer and it terrified me.

Mom said, "I don't want to put our lives in anymore danger. We've never been the aggressor and I don't want to put them on the defensive."

Adamos cleared his throat like he was about to deliver the most important speech of his life. "Time to be completely honest. Savvy?"

"Huh? Um, yeah, right." The list.

Mom leaned forward. "Savvy?"

"Well, um. You know Robert paid Constance a lot of money to bird watch at the monastery and search for a secret room? Well, he found it and stole scrolls but then he wanted out so drew a false map." I paused letting that information sink in before feeding her more. "Will's grandmother told me about a list. I'm thinking it might be in the monastery archives." I leaned forward. "And Constance told me how to find the room."

"What list?" Mom asked sharply.

"You don't know about the list?" I mean how could she? Edith was the one who told me. "The monks have a scroll that lists names, places, events, and dates of our families over hundreds of years. And all our crimes. They have sworn to destroy both our families. None of us are safe until we find it and destroy it."

"I had no idea," Mom whispered. "This can't be good."

"No kidding. We can't just run away and live happily ever after." I let that thought simmer for a moment. "Let me go. I won't cooperate until Will's family signs a truce. I can reveal the location of the secret room and we'll find the list together and then go our separate ways. When this is done, we can leave. They might be assassins. We might be spies. But we'll do our jobs with the promise not to strike at each other."

Adamos laughed and the warm tones washed over me. "You know, it's so crazy that it just might work."

"Let me go then." Mom sat down again. "You can tell me and I'll go in your place."

"No. You have to trust me. I have the relationship with them, not you." Tentatively I reached out for Mom's hand.

"I'm not just your daughter anymore. I'm your partner. And it's time to start treating me as one."

She hesitated, doubt flashing across her features before she pressed her lips together. She put her other hand on top of mine. "I'm in."

Adamos leaned over and put both his hand on top of hers. "I'm in too."

Thirty-five

MOM HEADED INSIDE, LEAVING Adamos and I in the backyard. The trees limbs were no longer shaped like jagged knives ready to rip into me and I found solace in the dark and quiet.

"Are you sure you're up for this tonight?" he asked. "We could wait a few days until you are rested."

"We have to move now," I said.

I couldn't look Adamos in the eyes. Everything he'd done for me had been about protection and keeping me alive. He knew about Malcolm, but I still held back a nugget of truth, an emotion that flickered inside me, betraying my mom and Adamos and everything they stood for. How could I tell him that I didn't want our mortal enemies to die? That part of my motivation in working with Malcolm's family was to stop this stupid war that stretched back hundreds of years. Plus, they had stolen the fake map off of Robert's body and I didn't want that to get them in trouble. Even if Will's family at some point turned on me, I wasn't going to turn on them. I couldn't face Malcolm again if I'd sent his family toward certain death.

"Talk to me." His voice was gentle.

"You know, Adamos, if you gave up the whole guardian thing and put yourself out there, women would be falling at your feet."

He shook his head. "Chasing after love is a fool's game. I had my turn. I promised not to love again."

It all came together. Normally I would bust his chops and let him know I'd caught onto his game, but I held back. This was too personal. If Adamos was using me as an excuse not to feel anything toward anyone then that was his choice. He'd lost his family and I knew a little bit about how that can change a person. And he'd really lost them.

He spoke again. "What is wrong?"

"Well..."

"If it affects our plan, you must tell us. I know you don't fully trust your mother yet but she needs to know everything you know."

"Fine, but it doesn't really affect our plans." I stumbled about with my words a bit until just spitting them out. "I don't want Malcolm's family to die. I know about our past, but I care about Malcolm."

Adamos let the silence sit between us but it wasn't awkward or condemning. He pulled me into a hug, which he rarely did, and the warmth of his arms and his solid body made me feel safer than I had in days.

He murmured in Greek, then said, "Little one, that's why I'm here. Because you care and because you're worth it. You saved me in Paris and I will someday save you."

Adamos pulled away and cleared his throat as if to shake off the momentary emotion. He picked up a black case that had been hidden under the patio table. "Let's get down to business."

"What's that?" The case almost melted in with the darkness giving it an ominous look.

He opened it with a click. I gasped. A shiny black pistol fit inside perfectly. I flash-backed to Paris and felt sick.

"No," I whispered. "No guns. I can't."

"I don't want you to go in unprotected."

"No guns. That's not what I'm about and that will put Will's family on the defensive. I'll go in with just my words and prove I'm there to help them."

Adamos put the gun away, nodded, and backed off. "You know best. Always follow your gut."

"Savvy?"

At the sound of Mom's voice, Adamos completely disappeared into the shadows to give us privacy. But I knew he was there ready to help.

"What?" I asked.

"Do you want me to come with you?" She stepped closer.

She was dressed in black, ready to go on a mission. Her hair sat in a bun on top of her head and for the first time she looked like Mom the spy, instead of just Mom. The hope and fear of a mission reflected in her eyes and she reminded me, of well, me. Maybe we were more alike than I thought. Our lives had been upended and we'd both struggled with surviving in this new world, and we'd both made mistakes. In that instant I forgave her completely. The anger drained from my body and I felt light, almost happy. I closed the gap between us and hugged her. When I went to pull away, she hugged me back.

"What was that for?" she asked, her voice filled with emotion.

"I forgive you." Then the words choked in my throat. I had my mom back. For real. And it had been me, not her, this whole time in Greece keeping us apart. I'd blamed her for not talking when my bitterness must have put up a ten-inch thick wall impossible to break through.

"Thank you," she whispered.

We stood like that for a few minutes. I just soaked up the Mom I'd missed. I didn't have all the answers to my questions, but in that moment I didn't care. Having Mom back was more important. I swear Adamos smiled at me from the shadows.

"Do you want my help tonight?"

I pulled away, a steely resignation settling on me. "I need to do this alone. For me."

She nodded. "As your mom, I disagree. But as your partner, I respect your decision. We'll be here if you need us. Just send out the call."

The house was dark and when I approached the front door to knock, it was open. All I had to do was give it a nudge and it swung on its hinges. It felt weird to enter uninvited into the house I'd lived in for weeks. In the darkened kitchen, I couldn't hear a sound. Where could they all be?

Prince trotted into the kitchen and I fed him some treats. I rubbed behind his ears. "Hey, boy." Why couldn't people be like Prince? Trusting, loving and only asking for a little bit in return. I rubbed behind his ears. "Good boy."

Thankfully, I'd crept through their house many nights in search of lemon bars. I knew every creaky spot on the floor, every spot where the moonlight streamed through when the clouds broke. I made my way to Bartholomew's office and couldn't shake the feeling that something was off. No alarms. No blinking red camera lights. I expected them to be home. I turned the doorknob and pushed it open, hesitating, listening for a sound or footsteps in the kitchen or outside, but there was nothing. I closed the office door behind me.

I fumbled in my small pack for a penlight. My mission was straightforward. Find the map and leave.

"I wondered how long it would take you to turn on us."

My head shot up. Edith sat behind Bartholomew's desk, her hands steepled, waiting for me.

"That's right," she said. "Quake in your boots because for the first time since you've lived under our roof you are now officially in enemy territory. You are now the enemy."

"This is not what it looks like." I dropped the penlight like it was a weapon. "I came looking for all of you, but when I got to the front door it was open..." I realized how lame that sounded. It totally looked like a break-in.

Her voice crackled with emotion. "I don't like or trust many people but because Malcolm liked you I was willing to try. You suckered me in hook, line and sinker. I just wonder if Malcolm knows what you're really like."

I cringed at the vitriol in her voice, the hatred and distrust coming off in waves. I didn't want to lose her trust. She might not like me much at all but she held sway over her family in ways I'd only realized over time.

"Please let me explain."

She waved her hand. "We should've listened to Will back in Paris and done away with you. But we didn't, because Malcolm said to hold off. Boy was that a mistake."

She clapped her hands and the secret room by the fireplace opened. Bartholomew walked out, a solemn look on his face. Janelle followed. She didn't even glance my way, but kept her head down and her hands folded. Will strode out, his steely eyes piercing mine.

Then Malcolm walked out. My heart leapt and I felt all tingly. He was here, really here, right in front of me. His eyes were shadowed by the lack of light so I didn't know where he was looking or what kind of emotion lay behind them, whether cold and dismissive or understanding. If he didn't believe my mission here tonight, then his family wouldn't either.

Thirty-six

EDITH RAPPED HER CANE on the floor. "We gave you the best of what we had—our boys. Malcolm saved your life. Will gave up his precious time to train you and this is what we get in return? You break into our house and sneak into our study to spy and steal?" She pointed her finger at me and accusation stung her words. "I shared my lemon bars with you."

I lowered my head and played with my fingernails. Would they even try to understand my reasoning? And I wasn't about to correct that she, in fact, never shared her lemon bars.

Bartholomew cleared his throat. "We've debated this long enough. Why don't we let Will have her and be done with it."

"Need we be so harsh?" Janelle asked. "I mean she is just a young girl. Maybe we should let her talk."

Will stepped forward from the shadows and sat on the corner of the desk.

"Young girl?" he scoffed. "When a young girl ruins the plans and infiltrates the top assassin family in the country I'd say she's not the innocent anymore." He turned to me, his eyes like small black holes, looking at me but not seeing. "Considering your ancestry we never should've given you a chance. We won't make the same mistake again."

The whole family murmured in agreement except Malcolm. He stayed silent, brooding from his spot where he leaned against the wall. He knew me better than that. But would he stick up for me?

"If you'd let me explain," I stated, trying to hide the fear.

"Not a good idea, dear," Janelle said, shutting me up.

Will crossed his arms. "It'll be my pleasure to eliminate the enemy."

The fear lacing my veins turned to anger and burned until I couldn't keep quiet. "Okay, that's enough. You guys weren't kind enough to do anything." My legs trembled. "You didn't take me in out of the kindness of your heart. That's crazy and you all know it. First, I wasn't really given a choice. When Will offered my family protection what was I supposed to say? No?"

Malcolm stiffened. I was glad he was here. He needed to know the facts. That I ran out on him not because I didn't like his plan or like him but I needed to follow through with my end of the deal so my family would be safe, so Constance would keep breathing.

I stepped closer to Will and as soon as I did all fear burned away, leaving me with the sword of truth and all I had to do was plunge it into their fabrication of twisted truths. I didn't let his glare unnerve me.

"And I was also offered training. Yes, I got into shape with some early morning runs and I learned some defensive moves, but then it stopped. Like you all planned to invite the enemy into your home, throw her some bones and then use her for her connections." I hesitated, wondering if I should reveal my thoughts behind their motivation. What the hell. "And you used me to bring your son home."

They all looked surprised and Edith gasped. "Bull rubbish, I say."

"No. It's the truth and you know it," I stated.

Bartholomew stroked his mustache and Janelle twisted her hands. Edith rubbed the top of cane and narrowed her eyes.

"That's right. At first, I thought you used me for my inside track with Constance but you didn't need me. Then Malcolm waltzed back into your home my first day of training. Coincidence? I think not." My confidence shot up and I felt like Sherlock Holmes or Ms. Marple about ready to break the case. "You hoped he'd return to watch over me, and you were right." I watched with satisfaction at the guilt that crept across their faces and the way they held themselves as if they were crawling back into their bodies. "But that's not where this ends."

"Oh no? Ms. Smartypants?" Edith said. "Well, please, don't keep us in suspense."

"I know Robert hired you to take care of Constance. But then you guys got greedy. You realized that Constance might be onto something with this map. And after I did all the dirty work, Will whisked in, killed a man in cold blood and stole the map."

"Pfft. That's nonsense, girl," Bartholomew said. "We don't kill anyone like that. It goes against the family code."

Will's eyes were like a red-hot laser beam, penetrating me, wanting to kill on the spot. The truth had been laid out as if on a rock of sacrifice, and anyone could see it and feel it pulsing with life. Will had broken the family code.

Edith broke in, her words sharp. "You think you're so smart, don't you?"

I shook my head, studying the wizened old woman who had been my nemesis, but also the one who'd finally told me the truth about the list and the real danger it represented to our families. "Sadly, no. It took the people in my life to help me realize what was going on because I was too close to see the truth. You laughed. You helped me learn to laugh during the moments in life when nothing seems to be going right." My voice cracked. "And for that I will always be thankful."

My words settled on them and they squirmed. Janelle broke down in a sob and moved forward to hug me. "Oh, dear we're thankful too."

"Mother." With the one word from Will, Janelle backed away, wiping her eyes.

"And that's why I'm here," I said.

"This is ridiculous," Will said. "We shouldn't be listening to this. She's working her charm on all of you again."

"No, let her continue," Malcolm said, speaking for the first time.

My heart surged with hope. "Earlier at the masque, Robert stole the map back from Constance. The same map that I'm assuming Will stole from him."

"You've mentioned that," said Will dryly.

"Robert thought he'd killed Constance, but in the final moments of his death, Constance whispered his dying secrets to me."

I paused, appreciating that the gleam in their eyes was one of curiosity and not I'm-about-to-kill-you. I lowered my voice for dramatic effect. "The map is fake and only I know the true whereabouts of the secret room, and," I struck a finger in the air and spoke louder, "that is where we will find the list."

Edith licked her lips and led the charge. "What do you want? Money? Gold? Jewels? Obviously you're here with some bargaining power." Her family nodded in agreement.

Here was my chance to stop this silly feud and bring safety to my family. "I propose we work together to find the list, destroy it, then come to a truce and go our separate ways."

After an uncomfortable silence, Bartholomew motioned the family closer. They conferred in a huddle. Their voices raised and lowered in passionate disagreement. Will's voice was louder than the others, and he clearly didn't trust me. Edith chirped in here and there, but overall, I had no idea what their final decision would be.

Finally, they separated, and Bartholomew stepped forward.

"We accept," he said. "But if there is any betrayal on your end, the truce is over."

I nodded, and we shook hands. They didn't waste time and huddled around Bartholomew's desk. He led the team.

"We cross by boat, dropping anchor far enough out that they can't see us. Then we swim." Bartholomew glanced around the room as if suspicious of spies. "We separate and infiltrate from different points. We'll each have a copy of the map and hope that one of us makes it inside. After three hours, we meet back at the boat. No taking chances."

"I hate to burst the bubble, but we don't exactly look like monks," I said. This plan sounded so crazy and full of holes.

Janelle reassured me. "We'll carry our costumes in a dry bag. We'll melt right in."

"Basically, it's each man for himself to leave the building and make it back to the boat." Malcolm drew the outline of the monastery on a piece of paper. "We'll work in teams and hope we all make it out alive."

My throat and lips became dry. It wouldn't take all of us to infiltrate the monastery and I didn't want it to seem like an attack. "No."

They all turned their heads, their faces puzzled, twisted into a question as to why I thought I could plan better than Bartholomew.

"Just Malcolm and I. We'll sneak in and then leave with the list and swim back out to the boat."

Will scoffed, his mocking laughter spurting out. "And why do you think that would work better, Savvy Bent? Please, enlighten us."

"We don't want it to seem like an attack. The more of us there are, the more likely they'll spot us. But Will can monitor the grounds and we can communicate with him if there's any trouble. And I trust Malcolm with my life."

"What if you run into trouble?" Janelle asked, probably more for my benefit than theirs.

"I know for sure I'm not killing anyone," I stated. If I was going to work with a family of assassins then that had to be established right away. "So we'll have to get creative. I'm sure we can manage."

"Savvy," Janelle said gently, "we don't take someone's life for fun or because they stand in our way. There are other means to stopping an enemy."

"That's right," Bartholomew said. Then he handed out black pens.

"What? Is this some kind of secret video recorder?" I asked. Because I knew it couldn't be just a regular pen with ink.

Bartholomew pointed the pen at the wall and clicked the top of the pen. Small electrified streaks of light poured out the tip. "It won't kill, but if you place it against the skin or close to it, the zap should stun him long enough that you can escape."

I tucked it away in my pocket. Sweet. Hopefully I wouldn't ever have to use it on anyone in this room. Bartholomew and Will stood to go, already discussing plans, in their element, their faces animated. An invisible burst of energy entered the room as the family nailed down the itty-bitty details of the mission.

Thirty-seven

I STOOD ON THE fringes as the family delved into assigning jobs in preparation to leave. Will would secure a motorboat since Malcolm's went kaboom into the great night sky. Janelle would pull the robes from their seemingly endless costume supply, and Edith would route the getaway, just in case. My job was the map and I didn't need to do anything but remember.

As soon as the plans were made and everyone was ready, we rushed out to the waiting car and zoomed down to the waterfront. The boat waited for us and we slipped through the darkness and climbed aboard.

With Bartholomew at the wheel, the boat sped through the water into the swirling darkness. The buzz of the motor drowned my thoughts but matched my nerves, which were at full throttle.

Time dragged on and yet it went by so quickly that when the anchor dropped, I was surprised. Will climbed down into the water first, then Malcolm and I. We had a dry bag strapped to our leg with our monk's robes. The cool water took my breath away but I went in without complaint. Then we were cutting through the choppy water at a slow but steady pace. Something I never could've done a month ago.

I kept my breathing at a constant pace, spitting out any water that sloshed into my mouth. The predawn glow reflected a path on the water that led to the monastery on the nearing shore looming over me. My heart beat faster.

Malcolm stood before I realized we were close. My feet touched solid ground and Will, Malcolm and I pushed silently through the gentle waves onto the rocky shore.

Were the monks kneeling at their beds or in the chapel by flickering candlelight? They were probably planning out their ultimate revenge and our timely deaths. I gritted my teeth together until my jaw ached. This would end tonight. I'd walk away with the list that condemned my family one way or the other.

Once on dry land and away from the shore where we could be easily spotted, we headed across the sparse grass. We hid in the shadows provided by the monastery and peeled off our wetsuits.

Except, when the suit flopped to the ground at my feet, I shivered. It felt like my last layer of defense, that my armor I'd been hiding behind for the last hour was gone. Wind pricked at my skin and the air smelled like rain.

Will spoke first. "Are you sure you remember?"

I nodded then focused on unrolling the robes from my dry bag and tucking the pen into the pocket. My mind was already searching the hidden cobwebbed corridors of the monastery while my heart was remembering Malcolm's boat exploding all over the beach, the flames eating up the sky, and the dark waters that I'd thought consumed him. The night our relationship changed forever.

We donned the robes, the rough material scratching at my still wet skin.

"Hey, are you okay?" Malcolm asked as he took in the monstrous building shadowing us, his eyes still not wandering my way.

I nodded, unable to bring up any words, not even to fake it for his sake or to hide my real fear, that at some point I'd lose him. Questions I had for Malcolm niggled at me, urging me to speak out and find the truth about that night. What if something went wrong on this mission? If God forbid the worst happened, I needed the truth. But when I went to pull on his arm, my arm wouldn't move, stuck by my side. He turned with a questioning look.

"What's wrong?" he asked.

When the moon moved behind a cloud so I couldn't see the contours of Malcolm's face or read his expression, the words I wanted to speak stuck in my throat.

Will interrupted, the disgust dripping off his words. "We shouldn't really waste time with small talk. You two need to get going. I'll be here on the outside, waiting. Please try and stay alive. This should be simple."

I saluted Will and then slid between the shadows of the monastery and the few trees while keeping close to the side wall, glad for an escape. I let my fingers run across the ancient stones, not wanting to accidentally pass anything. If Malcolm questioned my methods or doubted my memory, he kept them to himself. Once I reached the back of the monastery, and I couldn't find the change in the stones, I panicked.

Constance had said there would be a definite change in the stones; the once almost-even wall would turn broken and choppy, different stones jutting out as if not wedged in all the way, a mistake by the builders. But it wasn't a mistake. It was planned. Just as I was about to turn and study the wall, there it was, a definite transition. The hewn rocks became more uneven, enough for hands and feet to climb it.

I stopped and didn't dare look up or I might change my mind. With a few wraps of the robes, I girded them between my legs so I could climb without tripping. One false move and I'd go splat. Malcolm still didn't say anything but copied my motions. Slowly, bit by bit, we climbed the rock face. The rough stone passed beneath my fingers and feet.

Halfway up, I slowed, searching. Finally I stopped and forced myself to look up ahead. The end of a rope ladder swung in the gentle breeze. The fibers were dirty and worn and doubt flickered as to whether this was completely ludicrous and the ropes would tear under our weight.

I climbed past the end of the rope ladder, my fingers cramping, then with a deep breath, swung my leg over onto it and rung by rung continued upwards. Finally at the top I crawled through a window just large enough for a monk who didn't eat a lot. My stomach scraped across the bottom of it and I felt a hand on my back, pushing me through. Once in, I collapsed onto the floor, panting.

The dank smell that comes from years without sunlight assaulted me. Complete darkness swallowed me at the start of a tunnel that hadn't been used in centuries, except for Constance. I had no idea how he'd managed to squeeze through that opening, but I understood why he didn't want to do it again.

A few minutes later, Malcolm flopped down, his hand brushing mine by accident. My heart seized up at the warm feel of his skin against mine. The only sound was our breathing, the only thing I sensed was the heat from our bodies, the only thing I wanted was to be close to him.

We both rolled at the same time and our faces were pushed against each other. Accidentally, his lips pressed again my cheek, catching the side of my mouth. My breath hitched. I pulled away, my heart thudding.

"Savvy," he said.

As much as I wanted to talk, as much as I missed him desperately, I had to hold it together for the mission. I couldn't go there.

I turned my head and searched the inky blackness of the tunnel, then pulled away. "Let's go."

Thirty-eight

I HUNCHED OVER TO fit in the passageway and moved into the dark, welcoming its cool hug and the invisibility it offered me. Malcolm's soft tread echoed behind mine. I ignored the kiss of cobwebs against my face. Okay, I might've freaked out a little bit.

The dirt floor under our feet felt endless and the medieval monastery swallowed us whole as if it were the mouth of a giant creature.

Each step brought us closer to our family's safety. After about one hundred feet the passageway came to an end.

I felt in the darkness and pressed my hands against the part of the wall that dipped in a little bit, barely noticeable and cleverly disguised. I pushed and the stone swung open.

We slid into the room and when my feet touched the floor, I couldn't even see my hand in front of my face. If possible, the darkness was denser than in the tunnel.

"Hold on." Malcolm grunted. "There's got to be some kind of light. Feel around for a string or something."

I pawed at the air but came up empty.

"Found it," Malcolm said, followed by the click and then dim lighting from a naked bulb that barely cast a shadow in the room.

The archives weren't the grand library I was expecting. If a room were open to the public there would be tables and reading lights. This still had a dirt floor, and webs decorated the corners. Were those the red eyes of a rat gleaming in the corner?

I unwrapped my robes from around my waist and let the ends fall to the ground, a rush of air swishing across my legs. I slipped my hand into the secret pocket and touched the pen taser. I wanted to be ready.

Malcolm rubbed his hands together. "We made it."

"Yup. Now let's get to work." The words came out a little bit stronger than I'd intended. The responsible thing would be to talk about my feelings and the tiny flares of anger that came unexpectedly, but that would have to wait. I had to separate emotion from the spy mission and live and work above that.

He pulled scroll after scroll from the shelves, and I dove into the welcome work. I opened each one, searching line after line for a hint or trace of our families' names. I ran my fingers down the dusty scrolls just looking for last names because, of course, they weren't written in English.

Frustration mounted as I realized I still knew too little. We worked in silence and I tried to focus on the task at hand: the dusty scrolls and trying not to get too much mice poop on my hands. After about ten minutes, I sighed. Would this list even have a title?

"I don't think it's just going to be laying around unprotected," I said.

Malcolm moved to the farthest corner of the room and searched the cubbies. "I don't know about that. Come here."

He motioned me over and swept his hand up and down a shelf of scrolls. Cobwebs draped the walls and corner like the faded dress of a dying woman. A thick layer of dust decorated the top of shelf.

"Look at these. They're ancient." He glanced over my shoulder and then looked back at the scrolls, running his finger gently across them. "They're really ancient."

I studied the rolled ends filled with dust. Deep inside, I knew the significance of the scrolls representing the lost history and writings of an ancient time, but I cared about one scroll in particular. The one with my name on it! The one that offered freedom and safety for my family.

"Let's just find the list and get out of here." My conviction growing.

"Definitely," Malcolm said while gently pulling out some of the scrolls and unrolling them with a delicate touch.

I hovered, watching over his shoulder. He leaned close to the scrolls and studied the fancy inked lettering. "Maybe if we look for one that's not as caked with dust because I'm thinking they more recently added your name."

"Yeah, right. Not caked with dust." I pulled one out.

The dimly lit room encased us in shadows and I felt tucked away, hidden in another time, safe from the present. I fought against the overwhelming feeling that the list would be impossible to find as I pulled out scroll after scroll.

"Hey," I whispered. "What if we don't find it?"

I heard the shot first, then Malcolm groaned and slumped over, his full weight pressing against me. The warmth from his body that I normally loved turned into a suffocating heat and a gasp slipped between my teeth.

A dark figure crawled through the dark passageway in the wall and into the room.

Thirty-nine

I DROPPED TO THE floor and pulled Malcolm close, fighting against the tide of panic rushing through me. "Please."

"I'm okay," he rasped, but the way he held the wound and the pain flashing in his eyes told me he was anything but okay. "Fight," he whispered.

I lowered him to the ground. Then I stood tall and faced my enemy.

The monk's robes flowed to the ground and a hood hid his face. His fingers curled around a scroll, and he tapped it purposefully against his arm. His voice was heavily accented and he spoke in English. "Is this what you are looking for?"

The ancient rolled parchment clutched in his hand gleamed under the dim light, calling for me, asking for me to steal it. The list. He had the list. Time for my negotiation skills because I had to get Malcolm out of there fast.

"What would you trade for it?" I asked.

His voice turned solemn. "No trades. We need this. After we take care of the guilty parties, we will turn it in for quite a profit. Enough to make sure that all these precious scrolls are taken care of properly."

The lost scrolls? I searched for my pen taser but instead found a hole in the deep pocket of my robe. I remembered Will's lesson about using what you had. Unfortunately no sharp or heavy objects were nearby, but I had words and questions.

"This is about these old scrolls? Why?"

He shook his head. "You are like everyone else. The world hunts for these lost scrolls but not to preserve them. They want to get rich." He stepped closer, one foot at a time, and his words were as carefully measured. "But it is more than just the scrolls. It's the loss of life your families have brought to the world. We stumbled upon this list and fate brought our paths together."

I swallowed down the bitter pill that in many ways he was right. I didn't know half the stories filled with bloodshed and betrayal from the past two hundred years or longer.

He pointed a finger. "No one cares or they are greedy." He strode over to us. "These scrolls date back to Alexandria!"

I must've looked puzzled because he kept talking.

"The first library? Don't you know the story?" He paced, tapping the scroll I wanted against his hand. "Julius Caesar set the library on fire. Later, after Christ, many scrolls fell victim to the raging battle between Christians and Jews…"

He kept on with the history lesson, his words taking on a momentum of their own, his passion evident in the way he talked, the rush of breath, the shaky voice, but we were running out of time.

His words buzzed in my ear along with the urgency to do something, anything, to get Malcolm out of here with or without the list. His life, the beating of his heart, his family, and our hopeful future together was more important.

Any anger trapped inside at his disappearing act faded in light of the blood dripping onto the floor and the smell stinging my nostrils and the back of my throat. The time for words was over. I shot forward, aiming for the monk's legs.

He sidestepped and with one swipe of his leg, he took me out and I pitched forward. I turned in the air and my back hit the ground, breath shooting from my chest at the impact. He dug his knee into my stomach.

He pulled a long sharp knife from his robes and placed the blade to my neck. The cool metal felt like a light kiss against my skin. I didn't dare breathe. "We are very serious about our work here."

"What do you want?" I whispered.

He leaned close. "Vengeance is mine sayeth the Lord. And we are the Lord's right hand."

"No, you're just completely nuts," I gasped out.

The monk pulled the knife away from neck and lifted it above my chest.

Malcolm's face twisted with pain as he stood behind the monk. He brought the weight of his fists down on the back of the monk's neck. The monk fell forward and the knife sank into the hollow of my shoulder.

I cried out. Searing pain ripped at my body and the room blurred. Malcolm threw the monk to the side and their bodies twisted and writhed. I struggled for breath as the jabbing pain shot through my shoulder.

"Malcolm!" I croaked out, panic shooting through every nerve ending.

The extra effort caused more pain. I had to deal with the knife jutting out of my body. Blood coated my arm and the metallic smell singed the air. Tears wet my cheek, mixing with dust and sweat, slipping into my hair and falling to the ground. This wasn't how it was supposed to turn out. Memories flickered and faces of the people I loved flashed before my eyes.

I wrapped my fingers around the handle of the knife, and my breath quivered from my chest in anticipation of the fiery pain to come. With a grunt I pulled ever so slowly, the blade sliding from my flesh like a dull knife through butter and I threw it. It skittered across the floor and hit the metal bookshelf with a dull clang.

"Malcolm," I whispered, a sob releasing from my chest.

I rolled over with a grunt and noticed the tip of the pen poking out from beneath the shelves filled with dusty scrolls. I crawled over, ignoring the pulsing pain that told me to quit, to just lay down and accept my fate, Malcolm's fate.

With a shuddering breath, I stood, the pen gripped in my bloody palm. I zeroed in on the monk as he and Malcolm continued to struggle, one on top, then the other, their bodies a blur of movement.

My window came, a brief second, when the monk pushed Malcolm against the wall, trapping him, but leaving the back of his neck exposed.

I lunged and jabbed, pressing the top of the pen. I felt the vibration as the zap of power discharged into the monk's neck. He was stunned and spun around, a look of shock and distress on his face before Malcolm gave him the final push. He collapsed to the floor, his body twisting at an odd angle, his robes fanned around him.

I grabbed the list, which had fallen to the dirt during the fight and shoved it into a pocket of my robe that didn't have a hole. I turned in a rush and almost slammed into Malcolm but stopped inches from touching him.

"Are you okay?" he whispered, his face pale, with streaks of dirt on his cheeks.

"I'll make it."

We didn't move, leaning against each other and a bit in shock over how the easy mission had turned into a fight for our lives. Seconds passed. Time floated around us as we breathed each other in and tried to ignore the pain.

Malcolm pulled away first. "Let's get out of here."

His fingers looped into mine, and we limped toward the side. The gaping darkness that represented our escape seemed so far away and impossible to get to. "Can we do this?" The hole seemed too high.

"We have to." At the wall, he held out his hands. "Step here and I'll help you up."

I touched his shoulder. "But you're hurt. You can't do this."

"We'll worry about feeling hurt later. We can't afford to feel the pain. Now go!"

I winced and placed my foot into his locked fingers. "Ready?"

"Yup."

He lifted and I pushed off. My fingers were just about to scrape the ledge, when my balance was thrown off. The muted colors of the room blurred around me. I felt myself falling. Someone screamed, probably me. Air whooshed around me. I landed on top of Malcolm.

Pain shot through shoulder as I rolled off, groaning. "What happened?"

"I'm sorry. He knocked me over."

"What?"

Then we heard the scrape of rock against rock and the monk slipped through the secret entranceway.

Leaving us behind. And the exit sealed.

Forty

WE STUMBLED OVER TO the wall. Our fingers slid down through the dust as our fate became real.

I bit down on my lip and crushed it between my teeth until the pain was too much. The pen taser didn't have as much juice as I'd thought. The monk had left through the same hole we'd entered and then closed it off. I patted the list in my pocket but the victory was hollow. After starving or killing us, they'd prance in and take it back.

Fear knotted in my shoulder.

Malcolm's breathing was labored as he struggled to manage the pain. His chest rose and fell. His eyes were slits.

"Come here," I gently held his arm and led him over to the wall. "Let's sit and rest."

We slid our backs down the gritty wall until our butts landed on the floor. My shoulder throbbed and the blood slowed, drying on my arm. A crusty trail pulled and itched my skin. Malcolm's wounds had slowed but the blood still seeped through the rough material of the robe.

I tilted my head back against the wall. So many thoughts, ready to be spoken, but exhaustion covered me and it was all I could do to battle the panic rising in my mind, like how in hell would we get back to the boat. Malcolm seemed to sense my thoughts and squeezed my hand.

A whooshing sound echoed throughout the room followed by a clattering. I jumped and screamed, waiting for a round of chambers to be fired at us from secret holes in the wall but only dust floated in the air like dandelion fuzz in the spring. It filled my throat. We both coughed.

I searched the room. All the cubbies to the left of us had collapsed. All the scrolls and parchments were gone and the wooden structure lay almost flat against the wall.

A second whooshing sound followed and all the cubbies to our right collapsed, the scrolls disappearing.

"Holy hell," I said.

"Through the floor." Malcolm's voice was dull. "They released the bottoms of the cubbies and the scrolls dropped into a storage container underneath."

"What are they going to do with us?" I whispered. For some reason talking in a normal voice seemed wrong, like they could hear us and the very echo of our words would condemn us.

"Nothing good, I'm sure." He leaned his head back against the wall too and muttered, "There's got to be another way out."

Silence fell over us, the fear of death very real. I needed to speak my mind. I took a deep breath and the words tumbled out.

"Our families are a disaster, complete psychopaths," I hesitated, kicking myself at how horrible that sounded. "I mean we're separate from them. We don't have to be them or part of the mess that comes with them. Not saying we should completely desert them." I huffed, frustrated at my lack of clarity.

"Say it in English," Malcolm prodded. Pain crossed his face, his lips twitching and his eyes squeezing tighter.

I closed mine too and tried to clear my mind so all that was left was the simple truth. That I wanted to go back to the morning on his boat before I sneaked out, before it blew up and he disappeared. I hadn't been rejecting him but choosing my family, and Will had made an offer I couldn't refuse.

"I'm sorry. I never should've asked you to betray your family," I finally said.

"Savvy," he interrupted.

I held my breath and a tremor started in my arm and stretched to my fingers. He didn't reach for my hand, and my chest hollowed, all my hopes whooshing out, leaving nothing but my beating heart.

"We have so much to talk about." His voice was raspy and he breathed harder with the effort.

Before he could say more, the stone floor shuddered beneath us, sending ripples through my body. Deep in the ground, the choking sound of gears grinding and sputtering to life after years of inactivity vibrated the back of my legs. Hot prickles spread across my neck.

"Um, what was that?" I asked.

"Damn," he whispered, causing the prickles to run down my back.

The floor shuddered again and the wall pressed against my back, pushing me forward inch by inch. The wall was moving. My butt slid across the ground. I snapped my attention to Malcolm and the sudden stiffening of his back and the fear in his eyes.

Another shudder and groan and more grinding of gears and the wall across from us started moving toward us. Both walls were moving toward the center of the room. Inch by inch, slowly, the once square room was turning rectangular.

They had rigged the room with secret passages galore and fancy gizmos to protect their scrolls. They also rigged it to crush any intruders.

"Holy crap. Holy crap. Holy crap!" I whispered. Fear of death went to a whole new level.

He pushed to his feet, letting out a grunt of pain. I could see the influence of his family in the way he took charge, ready to find a solution. "I'll start on one side. You start on the other. Look for any kind of lever or switch to open a secret door."

Somehow, I managed to stand, adrenaline surging and overtaking the pain. The groan and creak of the moving walls pushed me to find escape. I shuffled along the wall, searching its surface for any kind of crack or crevice. I pushed, pulled, pressed and pounded. I tried to go slow but panic increased as we lost inches on the room every minute that passed.

"Any luck?" I asked.

"Nothing."

We kept at it, feeling and forging ahead. I coughed every few seconds at the dust stirred up by the moving prison walls. The grinding became a buzz in my ear as my frustration grew. This wouldn't work. The monks were too smart. Finally, we met on the other side, the room long and skinny, only a few feet wide. Our hands touched and we were slow to look at each other because then we'd have to face the fact and the fear that death was imminent.

"Savvy," he said, resignation in his voice.

But I wasn't ready to hear his words. I glanced at the other wall, only two feet away and closing. I'd never been claustrophobic but I trembled in the confined space. "How much time do we have?"

"Minutes," he said and finally reached for my hand. Just his gentle, warm touch brought a dull ache to my chest.

Scenes flashed through my head, all the ones I'd never experience. Seeing my family back together, safe and happy. And Malcolm and I, together, enjoying a regular date with dinner and casual flirting. Okay, and probably some kissing.

I did not want to die. Then I kicked myself. Since when had I given up on anything? "Where's the one place in the room, they'd absolutely want a way in and out?"

The answer came to us at the same time. "The scrolls!"

One foot away from being crushed, we scrambled to the end of the room where the oldest of the ancient scrolls had been kept. Frantically, we ran our hands over the wall.

I felt nothing. Absolutely nothing.

The gears kept grinding. The walls touched my arms and we had no place left to run. No time left for regrets, goodbyes or an I love you.

Forty-one

MALCOLM AND I LOOKED at each other, fear rising between us as the walls moved closer. His eyes were troubled and in their depths I caught a glimpse of the boy I loved, the one who rarely showed his true feelings. His guard was down in the moments before death and love, caring, fear, compassion all rolled together. He grabbed my hand while the other one kept groping at the wall.

"It's impossible," I said, the last of any hope draining out of me.

He moved his hand to the back of my head and pulled me forward. His lips crushed mine in a dizzying effect. The fear of dying and the thrill of his kiss crashed. If the taste of his lips was my last sweet thing on earth, I'd die happy.

He broke off our kiss, the cool air stinging my lips.

"Savvy!" His eyes widened and excitement flashed.

The floor dropped out from under us. My face scraped the sides of the wall as they closed together the last few inches. I screamed. Darkness swallowed me. My stomach pitched as I whooshed down some sort of slide, the air rippling through my hair and clothing. The cold, rough edges scraped at my skin and every time I bumped against the slide, pain shot through my shoulder.

I landed hard on my back. Stunned. I sank in and out of awareness. The pain was constant. Sharp. Shooting. Ebbing. Flowing. It changed but never left, constantly there, tearing at me.

New blood seeped from the closing edges of my wound, wetting my arm and leaving a cloying smell that mixed with the dank dusty scent of where I'd landed.

A scratching sound. Rough bristles brushed against my arm. I tensed, sending waves of pain.

"Malcolm?"

He had to be here. I moved my good arm and patted the dusty ground. Nothing.

"Malcolm?" I asked louder, my voice swallowed by the walls and smothering air.

Still no answer. I got to my knees and holding my hurt arm tight against my body, I crawled, feeling for the touch of warm skin, the touch of his clothes. I started to work out in circles, moving faster and faster.

The scurry of little feet of what were probably big rats would normally freak me out but I didn't pay them any attention. What freaked me out was that Malcolm was nowhere to be found. Nowhere. I spent minutes, pawing and clawing at the dirt, hoping, praying.

Finally, with my fingers sore and raw, I crumpled into a ball. My insides screamed. I sobbed and tears and snot flowed. My eyes swelled and I wanted to die right there. His family would never forgive me.

And when I could cry no more, I lay there, numb to the pain and the dark. And in that silence, the people I cared about spoke to me. With no fight left, my heart remembered. Malcolm whispered in my ear to not give up, that he hadn't sacrificed his life for me to die in the depths of a monastery. Edith's voice crackled in the air as she scolded me. A true heroine with grit wouldn't die alone. Adamos spoke to me. The soft tones of his voice spoke to my mind and soul, prodding me to fight. The memory of his voice soothed me.

And then my mom whispered to me. How could I let my dreams wither and fade when she still needed me? She needed me. She was on the outside, waiting.

I pushed aside the numbing hurt and pain engulfing me and dug my fingers into the hard-packed dirt floor. The monks always had an escape route. I started to the left and moved along the wall, swiping away cobwebs and ignoring the imaginary feel of spiders running their legs across my shoulders. As I moved around, the wall grew damp and when I moved farther my fingers came away with a bit of slime.

Water.

Where there was water, there would be a way out. Hope blossomed and I continued until the ground sloped upward. An opening? I pushed up, and slightly hunched, walked blindly through a tunnel with my good arm out in front.

Eventually a bit of light crept into the air and I inched forward, anxious for sun and the feel of fresh air against my skin. I moved one step at a time until small drafts hit my face. When the draft disappeared, I retraced my steps and felt the wall until part of the ceiling moved.

Dirt dislodged and dribbled onto my face and into my mouth. I turned and spit, while pushing. More dirt crumbled and slid to the floor. With one last big push that almost made me pass out, a trap door opened. Rain and wind rushed through, pelting my skin and whipping my hair about.

I found steps built into the wall and climbed out, then stumbled forward, trying to make sense of the sudden onslaught of noise and light. A figure rushed toward me, his arms outstretched as if to grab me, and I started running back to the hole in the ground. Darkness was better than a fight with monks.

"Savvy! It's Will." He whipped me around, the rain streaming down his face and dripping from his hair. "Where's Malcolm."

A sob blubbered up from my chest and I hiccupped, trying, but not able to speak the words.

"Where's Malcolm?"

I pointed to the hole. "The walls closed in, I fell, it was dark." I hung my head. "He didn't make it."

He ripped my robes off and ran his hands over my body, and he cursed when he noticed the wound on my shoulder. He placed his smooth hands on my cheeks. "Listen to me. I'll go find Malcolm. You go to the boat. My parents are waiting. Tell them to leave if we don't come back." He gave me a push. "Go."

"Let me go with you! I can help." I cried above the winds.

Will got right in my face. "You sure as hell can't help him in this condition. Now go!" He disappeared into the hole to retrace my path.

Clumps of mud oozed into the hole, torn up by my pushing open the trap door, which probably hadn't been used in decades. A draft of the muggy air wafted out and got sucked into the swirling wind. He'd told me to go the boat but I refused.

I saw the feathers first and thought a bird had swooped to take cover on the ground. But at my feet, an arrow sank into the ground, the end quivering in the wind. An arrow? I glanced up at the monastery, to the top, where a monk stood on the roof. Holy crap. A monk armed with a bow and arrows.

I grabbed my monk's robe that hid the precious list within its folds from the ground and sprinted across the shoddy grass and onto the rocky shore.

Forty-two

BARTHOLOMEW STOOD WAIST DEEP in the water, urging me forward with wild arm motions. The boat bobbed in the choppy waters. They'd driven it in way too close. For us. I glanced back at the empty opening.

The rush of water splashed up my legs and when I reached Bartholomew it only took him two seconds to evaluate my condition before he scooped me off my feet. The wind clawed at my face and the rain stung my wound. He pushed farther out into the water to the point it lapped at my feet. Bartholomew handed me to Janelle then he climbed onto the boat, and then together they laid me on the bottom on seat cushions.

A tear slipped down my cheek and dripped down my neck. Janelle went to work on bandaging my arm.

"Malcolm! Will!" I gasped out through the sting of the antiseptic.

"Shush now." Though I caught the apprehension in the line between her eyes and the twitch of her mouth.

They talked in hushed whispers, the words bumbling around me but never penetrating the wind. Finally, I shot up, causing Janelle to scold but I interrupted her. "We have to wait for them." She gently forced me back down.

Janelle nodded to Bartholomew and joined him at the front of the boat. He gunned the engine then let it settle down to a hum and pulled away from the shore. The boat lurched and pressed me to the side of the boat so my wound felt squeezed. Janelle didn't seem to notice as they both kept their backs to me, eyes looking forward out over the water, not even once glancing back to see if their sons were racing toward the water.

I grasped the side of the boat, my fingers in danger of slipping on the wet side and sending me crashing down on my back. With a last pull, my fingers cramping, I peeked over the side. The monastery moved up and down with the boat.

"No. We can't leave them!"

My fingers couldn't hold me and I crashed back down. My thoughts ran and coursed stronger than the pain. They weren't even checking back every few seconds. What if Malcolm and Will ran out, desperate for escape, and the boat was pulling away, with no one to see them? I couldn't think of one possible reason why Bartholomew and Janelle would leave them behind.

My next thought sent fear rising in my chest, stealing my breath. Were they going to dump me in the middle of the sea? They loved their sons, but they didn't love me. I was technically the enemy. Maybe a truce didn't mean much to them. Already I could feel the smooth fingers of the Mediterranean reaching up to pull me under, submerging me as water filled my mouth and chest, and the boat raced back to the monastery to pick up Malcolm and Will without me on it.

A convenient accident.

I scrambled to the back of the boat, pain slicing through my shoulder, but the adrenaline from my imagined death was stronger. With my good arm, I grabbed the First Aid kit, which had sharp, pointy corners. "I won't let you!"

The wind swallowed my words and the two of them didn't respond, unemotional and detached, straight on their path to the center of the sea. I sent a stronger message and hurled the kit. Instead of catching one of them on the side of the head like I'd hoped, it crashed down between them, the box ripping open and bandages and Band-aids rolling across the bottom.

Janelle gasped and followed the trail of gauze bandages back to me standing against the side of the boat, grasping the edge like I was hanging off a cliff. My body shook and I hoped I presented the image of a formidable foe and not a lunatic.

She laid her hand on Bartholomew's arm. He glanced back and immediately cut the engine, the boat slowing down until we bobbed in the water. The wind whipped my hair across my face and I swiped it past my ears.

"I won't let you kill me," I shouted.

Bartholomew stepped over the cracked plastic of the kit, moving forward, his arm outstretched. I bumped up against the back of the boat, ready to jump on my own.

"Savvy! Stop!" Janelle called out. "We're not going to hurt you."

I glanced between them at the hidden knowledge lurking in their eyes and the way they held their bodies. I nodded back toward the monastery. "Why else would you leave them behind?"

Sudden movement caught my eye. Then I whipped around for a better look. A head appeared out of the trapdoor in the ground back near the monastery. Seconds passed, and then another appeared: Will and then Malcolm. He crawled out and stumbled just like I did, blocking the rain with his arm.

"Malcolm!" I yelled.

Any thoughts of taking a dive into the sea left as the two rushed toward the rocky shore, waving their arms.

Bartholomew squeezed back between the two front seats, started the engine and raced back, drawing as close to shore as possible. The brothers ran across the grass, arrows flying, and then crashed into the waves. Will picked up Malcolm and pushed through the waters fighting his every step. He waited, the waves trying to knock them over.

The boat drew close and stopped. Will handed Malcolm over to his father who laid him on the floor. His hair was plastered to his head in clumps and his face was pinched with pain. He lay still, his ragged breathing sending out puffs of air in the cold. His face was deathly pale. I let out a quiet sob as relief filled my chest.

Bartholomew nodded to me and smiled. "We weren't leaving them behind. We wanted the monks to think we were all aboard so the boys had a better chance at escaping. They've been trained for this."

Then Bartholomew and Will moved to the front of the boat. The engine gunned once more and we were flying across the Mediterranean, water splashing into the boat, rain sprinkling our faces.

I slid to the floor, the adrenaline rush fading and a fresh feeling of safety taking its place. They weren't going to kill me. Janelle laid blankets over our legs and then whipped bandages and anti-septic around like a ninja. All the noises and sensation vibrated in my ears: Janelle yelling out curses at our condition, the roar of the boat fighting against the wind, the swaying and dipping motion wreaking havoc on my stomach, and Will yelling at us to hold on. Pain flickered like the monks were wielding their knives in the wound at my shoulder. It all faded, thrumming in the background and turning into white noise.

I couldn't keep my eyes off him, even though he looked battered and bruised with pink rivers running off his skin. I drank him in, every single piece of him. He was alive. Nothing else mattered.

He turned, his eyes finding mine and searching my face. "The wall closed on my robes, trapping me up by the opening of the chute." He answered my question before I could ask it and reached for my hand. He searched my eyes, his face softening.

I dropped my gaze to his lips and the drops of water clinging to them. My chest heaved with a sob, sending more pain through my shoulder. I reached out with my good arm and traced Malcolm's cheek.

He reached over, ignoring Janelle's pleas for us to lie still, and touched my arm. He moved his hand gently up to the back of my head and pulled me in for a kiss but halfway his chest shuddered. He fell back.

I gripped the blanket, wishing away the pain, for both of us, wondering if he would make it.

Forty-three

THE REST OF THE boat ride back was quiet and ominous, like the black storm clouds that hovered in the sky, following us. The bottom of the boat slapped the water and the wind created a tunnel of noise making it hard to hear anyone. Bartholomew glanced back at the fading view of the monastery. He'd look at Janelle and a silent communication would pass between them. But I didn't like the way his eyebrows were so low they almost hid his eyes or the way Janelle pursed her lips in a straight line, marking her face with fear.

I focused on the feel of our fingers intertwined, and Malcolm's thumb rubbing my skin. Every once in a while he tightened his grip and then relaxed it. While Janelle worked on his injury I tried to catch a glimpse of the gunshot wound but the bandages blocked the view. I'd have to wait until we got back to know how badly he was hurt.

When we reached shore, the family helped us into the car and we zoomed through the streets. I felt the urgency in the squeal of the brakes and the sharp turns that had Janelle yelling at Bartholomew to slow down. In front of the house, they helped us into Bartholomew's office. I lay out on the leather couch. Malcolm leaned back in the armchair. Janelle brought out a bigger first aid kit and replaced our bandages, her gentle touch reminding me of a mother's care. Relief crossed her face and she kissed Malcolm's cheek.

"Savvy, the wound will take time to heal but if you keep it clean, you'll be fine." She briefly smiled then turned to Malcolm and traced his cheek, but no words of comfort left her mouth, no glib comments about how the monk was a poor shot. And this, the fact she said nothing, squeezed my heart.

"Is the bullet still there?" I asked, wondering if she was quiet for our sake.

She smiled weakly, doubt glittering in her eyes. "Yes."

Fear shocked my core. As long as the bullet was still lodged in his side then he wasn't okay. "We've got to get him to the hospital!"

Malcolm shifted so he could see me. "I'm okay."

Bartholomew bustled through the room with a loaded suitcase in his hand, and a duffle under his arm. "Janelle!" he roared.

"Yes, yes!" she called out. She checked our bandages once more and then hurried off.

"You are not okay," I said.

The rest of my reprimand choked in my throat because I understood that the life of a spy or an assassin called for sacrifice, and sometimes, discomfort. Survival of the family had to come first, but the hurried frenzy of his family, moving in and out of the room, piling up bags in the room, made me worry.

"I'll get the treatment. My parents will see to that."

I nodded. Were they packing to leave? The questions about what that meant for Malcolm and I sent a sick feeling spiraling down through my stomach.

"Hey!" he said. "It'll be okay. Promise."

Promises. Always promises. A promise could only go so far. "What's going on?" I waved my hand toward his family still rushing, never stopping for a moment.

"We can't stay," Malcolm said. "They'll be coming for us, to retaliate. Time to get out of the country."

The truth behind his words knocked into me, leaving me gasping. I should've known. I needed to leave too, get away with Mom and Adamos and start a different life with Dad. Maybe Mom would leave since Constance was now safely off the target list. Just the thought of leaving Malcolm tore at my insides, my life splitting in two directions, and I couldn't go both ways.

"Hey," he said softly, his words sparking hope in my heart that he had a plan.

The door slammed.

There was a collective pause as we all froze. Then in one rush, Bartholomew gathered Janelle and Edith behind him. The point of Edith's cane flashed with the sharp blade. I stiffened, ready for anything, even the rush of monks burning with vengeance, their dark robes flowing.

But Mom burst into the room, a wild look in her eyes, frantically searching until she found me. She rushed over and took in my situation with one glance then with fingers twitching and a flush of red spreading across her face, she spit out words like a gun peppering the enemy.

"What did you do to her? What about protection?" she demanded.

Adamos followed her through the door and rested his hand on her shoulder, passing on a message with his gentle squeeze and the words he spoke that were too quiet for anyone to hear. Her face changed and the rage passed, her lips pressing together and her brow furrowed with the seriousness of her visit.

"They're coming. Now. Across the sea. Lots of them," she said, her words flying out and whipping through the room, stirring up fear and dread.

Adamos nodded in affirmation.

"We've got this all under control," Bartholomew boomed but the way he shifted from foot to foot and fiddled with his suitcase handle betrayed his words.

An awkward silence filled the room and I could feel the paranoid thoughts and theories racing and skimming along everyone's brainwaves. Including mine. I watched everyone, tension strung across their bodies like the string of a compound bow. Even Will had his teeth clenched, but as he worked his jaw, a battle raged on his face on whether to accept this help from his mortal enemy, in other words, my mom.

"We speak the truth." Adamos stepped forward and moved his arm to encompass the room in one sweep. "We're all in terrible danger."

Bartholomew snorted then hid his nervous smile with a fake cough. "And why should we believe you? You were one of them."

Mom stepped closer to Will. Her shoulders were back and her chest out, but I could see the slight tremor in her fingers. Distrust dripped from her face, a sneer formed on her mouth. The hatred between her and Will pulsed.

He mocked. "Nice to see you again, Marisa. Miss me?"

Mom had always been as cool and composed as a spy, never letting her guard down around me. But the slight tremor spread from her fingers, up her arms, down her body and to her legs.

He didn't give up. "Or maybe you're just jealous that your daughter trusted me. She is kinda cute. Very sexy when she's fighting."

Silence dropped in the room like a bomb. Emotions ran high and my adrenaline started pumping. A noise started in my mom's throat and built to a yell. She whipped something out of the side of her pants and lunged at Will, her scream reaching terrifying heights.

He deflected her with a sweep of his arm.

"Mom," I whispered.

"This is your fault!" she screamed at Will.

She jabbed at him with a knife in her fist several times while Will grabbed the nearest weapon, a pencil sharpener from his dad's desk. After Mom swung and missed, he countered and clocked her in the side of the head with the sharpener. She stumbled backward.

"Savvy, leave," Mom ordered, pulling herself together.

"You see," Will commented. "That's your problem. Your daughter came to me because I let her in instead of sheltering her. She's better off for it and that drives you nuts. Admit it."

"You stole years from my life." Her voice cracked yet she upped the volume a notch, bordering on sounding a bit mad. "You stole my family and memories. They haven't recovered!" Just as suddenly as the crazy anger had appeared it slid from her face and body language and then she spoke, her voice strong and determined. "She's been put in mortal danger, that's why she's here."

He laughed and mocked her with his casual body stance. "Please, I really don't want to hurt you, but if you continue I'll have to protect myself."

I moved off the couch and stepped toward Adamos. "Do something," I whispered.

He grabbed my hand. "This is your mother's battle. She needs this."

While Will was laughing, Mom backed off with her shoulders slumped. I wondered what the hell happened in the past that created this strange power he held over my mom.

"That's better," he said.

But then as soon as he turned his attention away from her, she lunged and drove the knife into his shoulder. Shock rippled across his face and the room. Seconds later Will pushed Mom against the wall. Didn't matter what he did, Mom fought back the best she could. She threw punches and kicks but Will was stronger.

No! No! No! I screamed on the inside. I didn't want to see our families fight. Too much was at stake. I hurled myself between them and screamed. Not just any scream but a shriek that would shatter glass in an ancient church, a girly teenage screech that would make old people cringe and babies start wailing.

Everyone froze and turned their attention on me, the one connecting thread who could bring peace to our families.

I ignored the constant throb in my shoulder. "Good. Now that I have everyone's attention, maybe we can act a bit civil around here." My voice started off weak and fragile, but as I drew from an inner strength that had slowly built over my time in Greece, my words became clear and strong. "Spies and assassins don't have to act like toddlers in the middle of a fight over their favorite toy."

Edith rapped her cane against the floor. "First bit of wisdom you've spoken since the day I met you. About time." She hmpfed. "Toddlers all of you."

"We need to leave the country." Bartholomew spoke the words with finality. He was agreeing with my mom and it was something he must've known anyway since the moment we left the monastery. That was why they were rushing around to pack.

"Well," I said, a secret smile tugging at my lips, "there's something you might want to see first."

Everyone stared at me, the questions in their minds apparent by the open mouths and raised eyebrows.

I grabbed for the robe, which I'd been holding onto like a baby would her blanket, then reached into the pocket and fished out a squashed piece of parchment. "The list."

Peace swirled through the room at the sight of the precious parchment in my grasp. Years of running, of being uncertain of their safety, disappeared, faded from their expressions, and slowly but surely, smiles spread, contagious, until Janelle giggled.

"Bartholomew, a lighter if you please?" I asked politely.

He scrounged in his drawer and handed it over. "Why certainly, young lady."

Giddiness erupted in my chest and I flicked the lighter, creating a small flame, representing hope for our families. I brought the flame closer to the scroll, the fire licking the air.

Two seconds later, a canister shattered the office window and rolled across the floor. Smoke hissed and released. I dropped the lighter and the scroll.

And just like that, hope evaporated.

Forty-four

THE ROLLING CANISTER CAME to a stop and then two more followed. Entrails of smoke rose in the air. Bartholomew sped into action. He pulled open a drawer hidden under the desk and tossed a gun to each member of his family. "For defense only. Aim to injure not to kill. Unless your life is in danger."

Will and Bartholomew pressed their bodies against the desk and with one giant heave pushed the massive piece of mahogany over on its side. Their actions were robotic as if they'd planned for situations like this over the years, each of them part of a well-oiled machine, working together, no doubt or hesitation.

"Suitcases are ready." Janelle called through the rising smoke as she dragged several of their suitcases behind the desk, her actions calm and rational.

"Great." Bartholomew smiled at Janelle, reassuring her that everything would be okay. "Mom, over here, now!"

Edith hobbled over behind the desk, just a cog in the wheel. She stood by the desk, waiting, with a calm reserve I wished would extend to me. Malcolm stood with his family even though his body shuddered with pain.

More glass shattered and shards scattered across the floor. One piece skittered until it stopped by my feet. Hands seemingly detached from bodies punched through the glass until the window was a clear opening.

With whoops meant to strike terror in our hearts, a flood of men in black masks poured through, a greasy black river tumbling, rushing, and covering the room. I pressed against the wall.

Smoke? I searched the room. The canisters shouldn't have caused this much smoke. A burning smell reached my nostrils. The carpet was on fire. Flames shot up off it from a blackened mass in the center. The scroll! The lighter! The two must've connected after the attack.

I coughed and waved at the smoke. Bartholomew and Will stood at the forefront, and the rest of his family, and Adamos and Mom flanked their sides forming a triangle.

Will ran into the attackers. He punched and kicked with precise aim to take them down. Bartholomew rammed the barrel of his gun into their heads, and they stumbled back. Before they could recover, Janelle shot at their knees, crippling them further. When one drew any closer, Edith jabbed her cane into their side.

The whirlwind of fear in my chest slowed and dwindled to just a few wispy breezes and surging in its place was determination. It filled my chest and sent what felt like supernatural strength to my arms and legs. This was it!

I sucked up any pain and stepped in line behind Mom and Adamos. Monks slipped through the cracks and attacked from behind.

I yanked a standing lamp from the wall and swung at any dark form that came near, taking them out one at a time.

Then I felt an explosion in my head as a fist connected with my temple. I stumbled back and bumped into Mom. The lamp clattered to the floor. She flipped around, and relief filled her eyes.

"Escape is the only option," she hissed. Her face came alive with emotion, her love apparent. "This is only partly our fight. I care more about us making it out alive. Go to the back bedroom and I'll meet you there."

"I want to fight with you," I mumbled as my head throbbed.

Mom gave me a gentle push then turned and kicked an attacker in the stomach. She brought her fists down on the back of his neck. He slumped to the floor. I backed to the far wall and inched my way along the edge.

A buzzing sounded in my ears and numbness vibrated in my chest. Ribbons of smoke twined through the room. The battle raged with grunts of pain and anger and the overpowering smell of sweat, blood and fear. The monks were contained but still fighting. Where was Malcolm? Was he hurt?

I dove into the middle of it, frantically dodging and ducking any stray fists. I spun in place and studied each and every face. Janelle and Edith were gone. Bartholomew, Will, Malcolm and Adamos were the only ones left still involved in the fight. They beat back the monks inch by inch. But it was the fire engulfing the room and the blast of heat that sent the attackers fleeing back through the window they'd entered.

I heard a weak moan off to the side, near the door. Mom sat on the floor, leaning against the wall, holding her side. "Mom," I whispered and ran to her. I hooked my arms underneath her and pulled her to her feet.

"No, Savvy! Save yourself. Go. Run away. Adamos will take care of you. Find your dad."

"No way. We're partners, remember?" I dragged Mom through the kitchen to my bedroom in the back of the house. My shoulder throbbed, and my mind was fuzzy from the smoke.

I slammed the door shut and brought Mom over to my bed. That was when I noticed the knife, still in Mom's grasp. I gently pried it from her fingers, then limped over to the door and leaned against it, my head tilted back. My eyes dropped closed and I became aware of the small things. The thumping of my heart. Each drop of sweat that slid down my face. The smell of blood that tickled the back of my throat.

And a knife clenched in my hand, stained with the blood of our enemies.

Forty-five

WE HAD TO GET out of there and escape into the night but my heart ached at what I'd be leaving behind. Mom lay across the covers, her hand still on her side, her breathing shallow. Blood seeped through her fingers.

Mom had been right about Will the whole time. He'd talked to her with such disdain and mockery, the hate reflected in his eyes. He probably enjoyed luring me into his family just to secretly stab at Mom's weaknesses: her relationship with me.

I placed the knife on the nightstand. With fast and jerky movements, I yanked opened the window and threw blankets over the hard edge to soften it for our escape. But one glance into the backyard and the multiple shadows surrounding the house and I slammed the window closed. The hard sound of wood against wood sent the truth spiraling through me. We were trapped. We drove the monks from the house only for them to surround us.

The door burst open and crashed against the back wall. Will staggered into the room, his knees bent and arms ready for action. Blood soaked his shirt where Mom had stabbed him earlier.

Smoke curled into the room behind him. Heat followed on its tail. Heat? Smoke? Holy crap. The fire had spread past the rug in the office. I peeked around Will and saw flames leaping into the kitchen.

"You," he muttered, swaying in a threatening way like he was about to charge.

My head knew what to do. Will had trained me exactly for situations like this except my body couldn't respond. In my mind, I saw myself grabbing the lamp and smacking him in the head with it.

"I really don't want to hurt you," I stated with a confidence I didn't feel.

He swayed closer, his eyes focusing on my mom.

I moved in front of her. "I suggest you find your family. But thanks for stopping in to make sure we're okay."

He waggled a finger at me and laughed. "You always were a bit clueless. From the very start you were like clay in my hands, ready to be what I wanted you to be. I expected a bit more of a challenge to be honest."

I slowly stepped back and with one hand felt for the lamp but I felt in slow motion.

"Just like your mom. Silly putty, the both of you. We should've done away with the both of you last year. But no," he mocked, "Malcolm had to go and fall in love or what he thinks is love."

He advanced toward me. His body tensed, and his face was a mask of anger. "And my little brother wanted to leave the family. Because of you." He pointed right at my chest as if his finger was a gun. "I'm not going to let that happen."

"If you hurt either of us," I threatened. "Malcolm will never forgive you and you'll lose him anyway."

He laughed and his tone needled the edges of my heart. The rational side of Will, the trained assassin had disappeared. Malcolm had taught me to keep my emotions in check, to not fight based on impulse, but Will was breaking all those rules. This was personal for him. Maybe because Mom had stabbed him, or maybe because she'd gotten away from him in the past. I'd probably never know the whole truth but I knew one thing: over my dead body would he lay a finger on my mom.

I flipped back the strands of hair that had fallen loose. "You're an ass. Jealous that Malcolm has a heart and you have a cold stone sitting in your chest that no one will ever love but your mother. And even that's doubtable."

"Savvy, no!" Mom warned, her voice weak.

He lunged and his arms wrapped around my legs. My back smacked into the small nightstand, the lamp within reach. My body buzzed. He whipped out a pistol and aimed it at my chest as he stumbled back toward the door.

"I'll tell Malcolm you said goodbye."

The black end of the pistol mesmerized me as I stared death in the face, like it had control over me. A dark flash entered the room. The pistol went off. The echo rang in my ears. I waited for the searing pain to enter my chest.

But the pain, the tearing of flesh and the blood never came. Will was flat on the floor, and the gunshot had exited through the window. Adamos towered over Will. Our eyes met. Adamos's were filled with love and strength as he slightly bowed to me as if he had now fulfilled his promise by saving my life.

Will grunted and moved. He rolled over and put three bullets in Adamos's chest. Immediately, blood flowed, and the dark red spread and stained. Adamos stumbled then collapsed to the floor.

"No!" I screamed.

The sad grieving part of my brain pressed to the back and survival instinct kicked up a notch. It was almost as if I stood outside my body watching. I grabbed the lamp and crashed it against Will's head. He deflected part of it with his arm. Pieces shattered onto the floor. I kicked the pistol from his hand and it skimmed across the floor and into the hallway.

"You bitch." He lunged again, his hands aiming for my throat.

At the last second, I grabbed the knife and held it out for protection. Will had his eyes on me, focused for the kill. He rammed forward and the knife sank into his stomach. He glanced down and then looked back at me, his eyes wide.

I gasped. Shock rippled from my fingertips and up my arm.

Pain crossed his face but he reached his hands around my throat anyway and squeezed. It only took seconds for my lungs to scream for air. Black spots danced in front of my eyes. I didn't have time to think about right or wrong. My hands still on the hilt of the knife, I twisted and shoved it deeper, stealing any chance for him to recover. Blood poured out and covered my hands. His grip loosened. I lifted up with my arms and twisted deeper and finally Will slumped over. I pushed him off.

Malcolm stood at the doorway, his arms resting on the wall, holding up his weakened body, his face a mix of shock and anger.

Forty-six

MOM WAS TALKING, BUT I didn't have time to read her reaction or figure out what she was trying to say. I didn't have time to figure out if I'd lost Malcolm forever. I zeroed in on Adamos and the curtain of red covering his chest. I rushed over and dropped to my knees. I stroked his hair and followed the line of the curl. Soothing words slipped out and covered him as I tried to keep him with me.

He tried to talk but gurgled as blood dripped from the corner of his mouth, then the words coughed out in spurts. "It's an honor. To protect you."

"Maybe we can slip through their line. We'll rush you to a hospital or Mom and I will nurse you back to health like before."

"This isn't Paris," he murmured.

I held onto him, my grip around him fierce and protective like if I held on tight and willed him to live then he would. The words built in my chest and rose, screaming through my throat but choking out in a whisper. "No!"

301

I felt the soft touch of a hand on my cheek, stopping the tears. Malcolm crouched next to me, his face grimaced with pain and he spoke with urgency. "The fire is spreading. We need to get out."

Adamos tried to move and groaned. "Listen to him."

"We can't." I spoke without looking at Malcolm. "They're waiting for the smoke and fire to drive us out."

Malcolm gently tried to loosen my hold on Adamos. "If you stay, you forfeit everything you've fought for. If you stay, his life, his sacrifice will be worth nothing."

His words hit home, tearing a hole in my chest so big it could never heal. I hugged Adamos one more time, not caring about the wet feel soaking into my shirt.

He mumbled.

"What?" I asked.

Malcolm tugged at my arm, pulling me to my feet. "Let's go. Now!"

I turned to Malcolm. "Get my mom. I'll be right there."

He glanced into the smoke and fire spreading to the kitchen. The giant flickering tongues licked the air, devouring anything it could find. "Fine." He rushed to my mom's side.

I fell back down near Adamos, studying his face. I traced his cheek and gazed into his chocolate eyes, memorizing every feature. "What did you say?"

He tried to talk but choked on the blood.

"Shh. It's okay. I'm here." I rubbed his arm.

He lifted his arm up to his neck and tried to grasp the chain of a necklace, fumbling with it. I pulled it out for him and found a locket.

"You want me to take this?" I squeezed his hand.

He closed his eyes, then opened them. I yanked it off and hid it in my hand, gripped tight. Then he groaned and his head rolled back. I put my arms around him, my throat burning with emotion, not caring about the blood or mess and kissed his cheek as his last breath wheezed from his chest.

"Thank you." I stroked his cheek. "For everything."

I pushed to my feet, swaying. My head felt heavy and my body sluggish. Adamos was gone. Already a dull ache resided inside, the part of me that used to feel safe, knowing he was always looking out for me.

Malcolm appeared by my side and slipped his hand into mine and squeezed. I barely felt it and didn't respond. My hand lay limp in his grasp and my stomach churned at the thought that he was touching the remains of his brother's blood.

Malcolm spoke. "Do you trust me?"

I paused before answering. Did I? Throughout all the games we'd played with each other, the times we hadn't trusted and made mistakes, in this moment, with kindness in his eyes, I trusted him. "Yes."

Mom cleared her throat behind Malcolm. "Our hands will be completely tied if we get caught up in an investigation."

Malcolm motioned for us to follow him. "You're going to have trust me on this one, both of you. Cover your mouth with your arm and try not to breathe the smoke. We have to go through the fire to reach the escape hatch." He covered his mouth with the crook of his elbow. "It's the only way."

"But," Mom argued, but I held up a hand.

"I trust him, Mom." And I moved into the smoke-laden room despite what logic would say.

We moved quietly and I looked away from the flames, the burning and collapsing furniture, and the memories. Smoke made it past my arm, filled my throat and stung my eyes. I coughed, and Malcolm moved faster, walking with a limp, favoring the side with the bullet wound.

"Duck down," he ordered.

We all scrambled through the hallway, crouched over, to escape the worst of the billowing black smoke that carried the smell of death. Mom gripped the back of my shirt and I held onto Malcolm's, and like a slow-moving train we made it to the office. The smoke was worse and half the roof had collapsed, some of the smoke escaping through the gaping hole. Debris and plaster lay on the floor, curled black from burning. Malcolm ran to the desk, stepping over the bodies littering the floor. The fight had ended and everyone scattered due to the fire.

"Down. Now. My parents and grandmother are ahead of us."

The escape hatch behind the desk was open and a ladder led down into darkness. A cold draft of air wafted up and I didn't hesitate. Each rung beneath my feet meant security for our lives. Mom followed and then Malcolm, who stumbled the last couple rungs. When we were all standing on the dirt floor of a tunnel, he pressed a button and the hatch closed.

He grabbed a headlamp from the wall, and then we stumbled down the tunnel. We didn't talk but stayed within the confines of our own thoughts. Sadness weighed in the air but I felt immune. Untouchable. Numb. I rubbed the locket tucked in the palm of my hand over and over. The smooth metal soothed me and kept my thoughts clear of emotion. This was the spot where Will must have lived, free and clear, and I understood why he kept himself free of emotional entanglements. About a hundred feet away, Malcolm stopped and I bumped into him. He groaned.

"Sorry," I said.

"Hey, Savvy," Malcolm whispered, the light from his headlamp flickering around the earthen walls.

"Yes."

"Do you really trust me?"

My heart fluttered. "Yes."

He looked at Mom and me, hope glittering in his eyes. "Are you ready to escape your lives? Start fresh?"

Mom waited for me to answer. I bit my lip. "What do you mean?"

"Kaboom," he whispered, his hands spreading, and that was all he needed to say for me to understand.

For the first time, I noticed the shadow of the black box on the wall and the wires leading back the way we came. The house must've been rigged for a quick escape, just like Malcolm was good at, like his tree house, like the boat. We could leave and no one would ever know who was here or what happened when our bodies weren't found. But doubt hovered and the dried blood on my hands, Will's blood, prevented me from saying yes.

Malcolm leaned against the wall, his hand over his wound. "Come here."

I leaned closer, his breath tickling my face. "What?"

His words were weak, his ragged breaths noticeable between every sentence. "It's okay. I saw everything. Will lost control. You were defending yourself. I know that."

My heart squeezed. I wanted to believe that his brother would never come between us.

"I'm serious," he whispered.

Love surged and broke through the confines of my heart. I thought back to our first date in Paris and the roller coaster my life had been since. I wanted new memories. My life, our future life together may not ever be normal, but we could be together.

Not caring that Mom stood right next to me, I leaned forward and grabbed his bottom lip with mine and kissed him. He reached his arms around me and crushed me against his chest, deepening the kiss. The smell of smoke and blood faded and hope drifted through in its place. My heart beat faster and the chords of love strengthened. The guilt flaked off in layers and the horror of the past few hours diminished, even though it had changed me for good and for bad, and I would never forget.

"Hate to break it to you two, but..." Mom's voice brought me back to reality.

Laughter bubbled in my chest and I couldn't help but giggle at the sweet hope of our future. But I had one more question. "Can we get my dad?"

"You bet. Wouldn't have it any other way."

"Mom?" I asked, reaching for her hand, asking her with just her name if she approved.

She hugged me and whispered in my ear. "I trust you. Something I should've done a long time ago."

Tears burned, fresh doubt rolling through my head. "What about your family?" I didn't have to mention my true fear, that their son's death would forever leave me the guilty party.

"They'll understand. He broke the code. Acted out of vengeance. They'll be devastated but they won't hold it against you, and if they do, then we'll break contact and disappear. I'm with you." The last part he spoke with great effort. He kissed the tip of my nose, his lips barely brushing my skin. "Forever."

"Okay, then. Let's do this," I said.

Malcolm got serious. He adjusted the light to focus on the black box and the red switch. "On my word. Run like hell. Don't stop. Got it?"

I stared into the inky blackness and the possible potholes, twists and turns that lay ahead of us, that could trip us up and foil our plans. "Where does it lead?"

He winked and kissed my head. "The future." He handed me his headlamp and nodded toward the blackness of the tunnel. "You take off. I'll be right behind."

"Are you sure?" I asked, not wanting to leave him behind.

"I'm sure. I don't want to take any chances."

I gave him a quick hug and Mom and I started down the tunnel. The dull light from the lamp flickered and wavered up and down as we ran. Seconds later, Malcolm yelled at us to run faster. He caught up and urged us on to our future, which lay just ahead.

We rounded a corner and an explosion deafened our ears as the past month or so and all the memories it held blew to smithereens. We slowed down and paused, panting, looking back at our past.

Malcolm leaned over and whispered in my ear. "Love you forever."

I kissed him, then whispered back, "Forever."

...to be continued in *Twist of Fate.*

Note from the author

Thank you so much for reading *Heart of an Assassin*.

Thanks for taking this journey with me. I'm so grateful for all my readers. I appreciate you! I couldn't do this without all of you.

I'd love to hear from you. You can contact me through the contact tab on my blog at laurapauling.com.

Also by Laura

Circle of Spies Series

A SPY LIKE ME - Book 1

HEART OF AN ASSASSIN - Book 2

VANISHING POINT - a novella - Coming fall 2013

TWIST OF FATE - Book 3 - Coming fall 2013

Other works

HEIST - a time travel thriller

About Laura Pauling

Laura writes about spies, murder and mystery. She's the author of the exciting Circle of Spies Series, and the psychological thriller, HEIST. She's a former elementary teacher and currently lives in New England. After spending time reading books to her kids and loving a good plot turn, she put her fingers to the keyboard. Don't ask her about the unfinished quilts and scrapbooks. Stories are way more exciting. She writes to entertain and experience a great story...and to be able to work in her jammies and slippers.

Visit www.laurapauling.com for more information on her books and to sign up for her newsletter.